Pride & Precedents

KATHERINE E. WEBB

This is a work of fiction. Names, characters, places, and incidents either are the product of the author's imagination or are used fictitiously. Any resemblance to actual persons, living or dead, events, or locales is entirely coincidental.

Copyright © 2024 by Katherine E. Wright

All rights reserved.

No portion of this book may be reproduced in any form without written permission from the publisher or author, except as permitted by U.S. copyright law.

Contents

This book is dedicated to everyone who has overcome the trauma and mistakes of their past to blaze their own trail to happiness and fulfillment.

Author's Note

This book contains depictions of cheating and disordered weight & body thoughts. Racism, the death of a parent, and an accidental pregnancy are also addressed. If these topics are triggering for you, please proceed with care.

CHAPTER ONE

Prologue

HENRY

March 13th, 2009

I take one final look in the mirror to check the buttons on my Henley shirt. *Shit. Should I leave one open to show off my chest hair, or keep it classy?* Naomi's never had a problem with what I wore before... Considering all our previous hookups have been sandwiched between my crew practices, her orchestra rehearsals, and our Constitutional Law study sessions, fashion hasn't really been a priority. The last time we got together, I was still in my sweaty gym shorts, for Christ's sake.

That she's so low-maintenance is one of my favorite things about Naomi. That, and she's an actual genius. She strutted into class and sat in the very first row, right next to me. While everyone else had their laptops open, she went old school with a legal pad and a dictaphone. She radiated confidence, which she promptly backed up when she raised her hand to answer all the professor's questions; a professor known to take content from every part of the textbook, even the footnotes. In a word, she was intimidating. I committed myself to work harder, study longer, worried she might knock me out of the top spot with her brilliance. And then our eyes locked, and all thoughts of school work flew from my head.

Naomi is a certified ten. I'm tall at 6'2", but she's no slouch herself at 5'10". She says her long, sinewy limbs are her secret weapon for playing the cello, and since he's been the first chair cellist in the Yale Symphony Orchestra since our first year, I'll take her word for it. Bone straight, raven hair spills over her shoulders and reaches all the way past her butt, which is small, but perky and accentuated by the miniskirts she wears on a near daily basis. And as a breast man myself, I'm more than satisfied with her ample handful. She's like my own personal Sailor Moon...if Sailor had black hair instead of blonde.

She might not care about clothing or whether I text her before bed, but today, she gets the full gentleman experience. I told her we needed to link up to compare notes for next week's exam, but actually, I'm finally gonna take the dive and ask her to be my girlfriend.

I've been thinking about it for a while—how I almost itch when I go a whole day without seeing her, how I get bummed when she goes back to her apartment instead of staying over at mine, how even slogging through our mammoth Chemerinsky textbook isn't enough to keep me from getting hard around her. Nearly one-hundred pages on Economic Liberties should be able to tame the beast, and yet, when Naomi's around, I'm adjusting myself and blushing like a horny teenager with a crush.

At first, it was embarrassing—and not ideal for studying—until I realized she was just as turned on as I was. We'd been study partners for three weeks—*Thank you, Professor Feinstein!*—and she was sitting so close on my hand-me-down couch that our knees were touching. I thought I was hiding my reaction to her until I caught her staring at the prominent ridge in my pants. Her dark, almond eyes were wide, her delicate lips were parted, and she had stopped talking mid-sentence. The rosy tint in her cheeks was unmistakable when she looked up to meet my eyes.

But instead of playing coy, she'd surprised the shit out of me by pushing her books off her lap and launching herself at me lips-first. She tasted so luscious when her tongue slipped into my mouth, felt so perfect in my arms that instinctively slid around her waist. I was in shock for a full five seconds while my brain caught up with my body, and then I was kissing her back passionately, squeezing her butt until she breathed soft moans against my lips, grinding her obvious wetness against my thigh.

That was two months ago. Two months of quickies in the stacks, make out sessions in the boathouse, and me, slowly but surely, falling for her.

A few weeks ago, I made the mistake of telling my twin, Noah, about my feelings. He made fun of me mercilessly, saying our old school Korean dad would never allow his eldest son to bring home a Japanese woman, but we both know that's bullshit. Dad might be old school when it comes to acceptable career paths and chivalry, but he and Mom have always been progressive when it comes to relationships. Besides, he could hardly get upset about me dating a Japanese girl when he married a White woman. None of that stopped Noah from changing his Caller Tune to Devo's "Whip It". *Asshole.*

But I'm getting ahead of myself. First, I have to make things official. *Then* I can worry about whether she could handle Thanksgiving at the Park house with all four of my brothers. I take a deep breath, nervously finger comb my hair for the thousandth time, grab my keys, wipe my sweaty palms on my jeans, and head out the door.

It's a short walk to her apartment; she lives in the Park Street district, and I'm practically right around the corner in the Chapel Street area. We could be even closer if we moved in together...Maybe next year? *Slow your roll, Henry You don't even know what she's going to say.*

Before I've had a chance to calm my nerves, I slip inside as another tenant exits and make my way to her front door. *Flowers! I should've brought flowers! Maybe that would've seemed too thirsty? Fuck it. I'm already here.*

I have to knock twice before I hear any movement inside. That's unusual, considering I texted her last night to remind her about our study session. I hear more muffled stumbling before the door is thrown open.

It's not Naomi. Not her roommate. Standing in front of me, wearing nothing but boxers and a lopsided grin is Tanner, my teammate from crew. *What the fuck?! What is he doing here? What is he doing here* half naked?

Against my will, my brain tallies up all the details before me. Tanner's douchebag face looking sweaty, flushed, and *smug*. Maxwell music coming out of Naomi's open bedroom door. Clearly, I've misread things. Here I thought we were on track to make things official, and she thinks it's the perfect time to start hooking up with my fucking *teammate*.

I go cold and numb immediately, like when I fell through the ice on our last family trip to Promised Land State Park. Sure, it would be satisfying to wipe that smug look off Tanner's face with my fists, but no one's gonna hire someone with a law degree from Yale and a felony assault on his record. After momentary rage, I feel myself shutting down further, closing off those useless, touchy-feely parts of myself that allowed this disaster to happen to me, allowed me to feel this...*hurt*.

I hear Naomi's sweet laughter clearly through the open door.

"Who is it, Tan, babe? Can't you tell them we're busy?" Tanner's smug grin turns wicked. He knew I liked Naomi. He almost caught us in the boathouse once. He took one look at me with my fly open and her with her skirt pushed up and backed out slowly, but not before raking his eyes up and down her body like the asshole he is. He wanted her, and he didn't care that she was mine.

But she wasn't mine. Not really. She was just my almost-girlfriend and now, first heartbreak. All I was to her was a study partner and occasional lay.

I walk away from the still open door without saying a word. What's there to say? In two more weeks, this class will be done, along with our second year. Sure, I'll see her around next year, but it's mostly electives and we luckily don't have the same specialty. Just two more weeks, a few awkward meetings around campus, or maybe while grabbing groceries at Shaw's, and then I never have to see Naomi again.

CHAPTER TWO

Henry

"Ms. Sanchez! Do you have a moment?" I shout through my cracked office door. There's no point in bothering with the intercom when 80% of the office has already gone home. Mere seconds later, Ms. Sanchez—*Camila* to the rest of the office—strides through my door with a look on her face that indicates she's *thrilled* to be summoned at this hour. Her generous hips are cocked against an armchair in my office's seating area, her full lips are pursed, and she taps her emerald green gel pen against the legal pad in her arms impatiently. She is the very picture of irritated.

As one of the best paralegals in the firm, she's earned the occasional attitude. Every other department would snatch her up in a heartbeat if I made the mistake of letting her go. I basically stole her from Jonathan when she filled in for Vanessa, my last paralegal, all those years ago.

Vanessa was perfectly fine. She got the job done exactly as I asked, and no further. It wasn't as overt as *malicious compliance*, she just... She never went the extra mile to show me she actually *cared* about the work we do in Divorce, one of the most lucrative departments at Bannister, Banks, Smith & Park. Lucrative enough for me to make partner and top the billable hours list for six years running, but apparently not lucrative enough for her to take any initiative.

Sure, Vanessa never complained when I asked her to work through lunch or stay late to prep for a mediation between a celebrity chef and his young, sexy, ambitious, soon-to-be ex-sous chef/wife, but she also never asked any questions about the clients that weren't *absolutely necessary*, never surprised me with potentially game-changing research on new alimony payment structures or prenup clauses, and barely used any of the professional development resources provided by the firm.

While no one in their right mind would describe my management style as "warm and cuddly", she also never even tried to connect with me as a *person*, offering to pick up coffee when she made a Starbucks run, or bringing in cupcakes for the breakroom on my birthday. Those things aren't technically a paralegal's job, but plenty of them do it.

Basically, she was the complete opposite of Camila in all the wrong ways.

All of that was fine—not *great*, but *fine*—when I was an associate and junior partner, paying my dues with annulments, then summary divorces and uncontested filings, and then playing second fiddle on some of the more complex cases. But when I was promoted to partner seven years ago, I knew I needed someone as high-performing as I was. Someone trying to make a name for themselves, even if they aren't gunning for the partner track.

I'm basically a shark around here, which earned me the nickname "Sub Zero", though no one has been stupid enough to call me that to my face. When I first overheard the moniker, it felt borderline racist to be the only Asian partner in the firm and named after an Asian character in Mortal Kombat, but honestly, the name fits. Top billable hours six years running means if you cheated on your pregnant wife who had the forethought to demand an ironclad prenup with a fidelity clause, seeing me across the conference room table or courtroom aisle is your worst nightmare. Overflowing with satisfaction but still maintaining my ever present composure, I've seen seasoned veterans break out in a sweat at my arrival.

Unfortunately, it also means less than forty hours of sleep (*total*) most weeks, lots of missed dates and appointments, and a truly dismal social life. *Can a social life be dismal if it's nonexistent?* I barely manage to make time for weekly dinners with my family in Brooklyn, especially since I moved out to Westchester four years ago, but Mom and Dad would have my hide if I even thought about bailing. Luckily, the commute means I can make up the time on the drive in when I don't opt for the Metro North.

But that's not the only reason they call me "Sub Zero". Around the firm, I've got a reputation for being ice cold and a stickler for the rules—in law and in the workplace.

- *Tardiness is unacceptable.*

- *Proper titles and formal greetings are a sign of respect.*

- *Wrinkles, stains, and messiness of any kind have no place in the office.*

- *No personal calls at the office.*

- *One month's notice is required for any time off from work.*

- *No romance in the workplace, whether with clients or colleagues.*

- *No heating seafood up in the office microwave.*

That last one is just common sense, but it doesn't stop the office manager from having to send an e-blast to all staff (at my request) almost every month because someone just had to bring their leftover crab cakes to work. *I'm sure they're delicious, Jennifer, but no client appreciates smelling day old fish when they're getting billed upwards of $1000 an hour.*

When Vanessa got back from her honeymoon—which she took with only *three weeks'* notice—I'd already gotten used to Camila's stellar attention to detail, frequent and incisive questions about clients and legal precedents, and constant willingness to go above and beyond. Her work ethic put even some of the junior associates to shame. I hardly knew anything about her,—which I loved, considering I prefer not to get too personal in the office—but I knew she was the kind of paralegal a full partner would need by his side. Luckily for me, I had (and *still have*) seniority over Jonathan and was not afraid to pull rank. Camila stayed with me and Vanessa went back to the firm's *second best* divorce attorney instead. I'm not even sure if she's still with the firm, but Jonathan and I have been in a bitter rivalry ever since. A rivalry he has no hope of winning.

I look up at my right-hand woman, tapping her pen and awaiting the latest assignment that will likely have her tied up in paperwork for another two hours, minimum.

"I'm waiting with bated breath, Henry."

My gaze hardens slightly. Occasional attitude is one thing, but she knows how I feel about proper titles. She shifts on her feet and lets out a disconcerted puff of air before squaring her shoulders and making direct eye contact.

"My apologies, *Mr. Park*. How may I help you?"

Decorum once again restored, I stand up from my chair and feel a soft pop in my lumbar vertebrae; it may be the first time I've come up for air since my three o'clock meeting. I pace a few steps, then settle against the edge of my desk with my arms folded.

"At lunch today, Mr. Bannister," one of the firm's two founding partners, "gave me a heads up that they're bringing in a potential VIP client that I have to woo at a 9:00am 'meet and greet' tomorrow. That gives us less than twelve hours to create full dossiers on the couple, though Bannister's office already ran a full background check. The wife is apparently a lawyer too and just relocated from San Francisco for a job in the city, so we have to ensure all of our work can pass white glove inspection. There can't be any shortcuts with this one."

As if either of us would *ever* take shortcuts. The whole time I've been speaking, Camila's been taking detailed notes, giving me her full attention.

"If she's a lawyer, I'm assuming she has a colleague who could handle this rather than take us up on retainer?"

A very common practice. Once again, she proves to be the perfect paralegal. I barely control the smile tugging at the corners of my mouth.

"Apparently her counsel is close with the husband and she didn't trust that he would be impartial. Then, with the job offer and relocation, she needed counsel based in New York." Camila pauses writing and raises a perfectly manicured eyebrow.

"You've said twice that *she* relocated. Did the husband stay behind?" My mouth gives up and lifts into a tiny smirk.

"Apparently, he's months away from an IPO, which means he's tied to his company and San Francisco until those shares drop." Camila stops writing abruptly and her mouth drops open.

"She's filing for divorce during the run-up to an IPO? That is cold-blooded."

Cold-blooded and a potential handicap in whatever settlement we can reach, but we'll know more when we learn how he contributed to the petition to divorce.

"We won't know how big a problem that is until we get more details on the marital situation." I move back around my desk and take a seat, my cue that the conversation is over. Camila takes the hint and flips down the pages on her pad. On her way out, she stops suddenly.

"Wait a minute! What are the names of these VIPs?"

I don't bother looking up from my now open browser. "Mr. Bannister didn't want to risk getting into details while out at lunch, since the news of the divorce filing isn't yet public. Can you stop by his office and get the names from his paralegal before you get started? I'll be meeting my car in the next thirty minutes, but, as always, I'm reachable. I'll expect the dossiers in my inbox by 7:00am tomorrow morning." She nods.

"On it." With a slight sway of her hips, she turns on her sensible heels and heads out of my office, closing the door behind her.

Though capable, fashionable, she is *not*. I've never seen her in heels higher than two inches, her skirt suits are clearly cheap,—it'd likely take ten to match the price of just *one* of my suits—and she never bothers much with makeup or fussy hairstyles. Even with all that, she's not unattractive, but her wardrobe is the one area where I wouldn't mind some improvement.

Not that she's an extension of me, but a paralegal could be a *reflection* of me. What does it say to the opposing party, to potential clients, that my paralegal is so...dowdy? Especially taking into account how sharply I dress,—my body touches nothing but Brooks Brothers, Brioni, Brunello Cucinelli, and Zegna—the difference is striking. Her cheap clothes, lack of makeup, and general frumpiness don't violate our firm's dress code, however, and I'm not about to risk a discrimination lawsuit making unsolicited comments on a female employee's appearance.

My phone buzzes next to my keyboard.

Murray

Your car is out front, sir.

Murray's been my driver ever since I made the move out of the city. He's demonstrated outstanding professionalism since Day 1. He doesn't chatter needlessly during the drive, he knows when to raise the privacy screen without me even having to ask, and he's perpetually five minutes early.

I grab my suit jacket from the back of my chair and put it on, tuck my crucial papers into my briefcase and snap it shut, turn off my desk and office lights, and finally lock the door behind me. I trust Camila will have the requested documentation ready in time for my review tomorrow morning.

Chapter Three

Camila

Goddamnit! I was almost home free! I haven't gotten out before 8:00pm in going on two weeks now. Add that to the subway ride home, and I'm lucky if I see my bed by 10:00pm most nights. Note to bosses everywhere: *Work-life balance shouldn't just be for the partners and C-suite!*

I allow myself a few more seconds of ineffectual grumbling before flipping to a fresh page in my trusty legal pad and making my way down to Mr. Bannister's office. Some paralegals take notes on their phones, but I worry it looks like I'm texting, so I stick to the tried and true methods. I pass a few more vacant offices before reaching Mr. Bannister's reception area. Poor Cici, his beleaguered paralegal, has got to have a cot hidden somewhere as late as she works. She looks up from her computer and nods in silent greeting.

"Hey Cici, girl. Mr. Park just sent me to get the names of the potential VIP petitioners. I need to put together full dossiers for both by tomorrow. Did Mr. Bannister, perhaps, leave them with you?"

Cici leans back in her chair before starting to search her desk.

"Let me see..." She pushes back ginger bangs that come loose from her chignon as she opens and closes a few drawers. That is exactly why I stick with a bun and barrettes. Long hours, law school, and doing my best not to completely neglect my family obligations leaves me no time for hairspray, curling irons, or fabrics that can't stand up to a mustard stain after another lunch at my desk. I barely have time to shower some days. My work outfits are basically a uniform; I've got three of the same suits in two different colors to cover the whole week. Cici sighs and shakes her head, her search obviously coming up empty.

"No dice, Camila. I'll let him know you're here, though."

I nod and take a seat in the waiting area. I rub the stiffness out of my ankles, roll my shoulders, and let my thoughts wander to my overbearing overlord.

Henry's been wound tighter than usual lately, and that's saying something for a man who's basically a cyborg. A *painfully sexy* and incredibly successful cyborg, but still. My guess is either he's got one too many clients,—six straight years as the firm's top earner has got to start taking a toll on you at *some* point—or he seriously needs to get laid. Considering he's either here working late with me, working from his car, or working from home, he's likely had as much sex as I have in the last few months: nada.

All work and no play makes Camila a dangerously pent up girl. I sigh and push useless thoughts of sex (or lack thereof) to the back of my brain.

I normally don't have a problem staying late. What else can you expect when you're a paralegal for one of the partners at a firm that's been ranked in the top five of US News & World Reports' Best Law Firms ten years and counting? That's not just best firms in *NYC*; that's best firms in the *country*. I was just *really* hoping to knock out my last mid-term (ever!) so I could start focusing on studying for the bar and finally make the leap from overworked and underappreciated paralegal to full-fledged attorney.

Not *here*, of course. Syracuse's JDinteractive program is impressive,—my little sister, Aurora, surprised me with a legit cake from Carlo's when I got in, and then my baby brother, Gabriel, took us out for way too many Harvey Wallbangers—but I doubt it'll get the attention of the higher ups at Bannister, Banks, Smith & Park. That's why I've kept the fact that I've been working towards my J.D. for nearly five years a secret from everyone at the firm. What I do outside of work is none of their business; I'm just glad I found a program I can do when I don't know whether I'll get home by 8:00pm or midnight. Once I pass the bar and have an entry-level gig lined up (maybe something in Entertainment Law), I'll be giving my one month's notice.

God, *five years*! This program has been an absolute *beast*. I pride myself on being a competent woman with an abundance of grit,—my mom worked hard to give that to all her

children, despite growing up in projects-adjacent housing in the
Bronx—but there were times I thought even *I* couldn't handle
everything. I'll probably sleep for a week when this is all over.
Thoughts of my mom swirl in my head and I start absentmind-
edly tapping my pen.

Valentina Sanchez raised her children to be smart, strong,
and proud of their Puerto Rican heritage, no matter how many
zeros were in our bank account, or how many times a week
we had *arroz con pollo*. We didn't get private schools, expensive
extracurriculars, or fancy summer vacation plans, but we did get
a home life full of love and attention, and a mother who believed
we could do whatever we wanted to do. She gave everything
so we could be successful...until she fell asleep on the bus ride
home from work and never woke up.

The doctors said it was a pulmonary embolism. Apparently,
all those headaches *were* worth a visit to the doctor. I'd been
in my junior year at CUNY, and suddenly *I* had to step into
the role of single parent for two younger siblings. The grief was
unbearable, and I lost my streak on the Dean's list in all the
fallout. But I finished.

Instead of going to law school right after college,—that
would hardly have been possible with the way my grades tanked
anyway—I got my paralegal certification and landed a job with
Bannister, Banks, Smith & Park to make ends meet and learn as
much behind the scenes as I could. And though I'm nowhere
near the mother my mom was, we kept the apartment, Gabriel
finished high school and started at Fordham, Aurora finished

college (*she even got a scholarship to NYU for film school!*), and life started to even out again. Five years to finish law school definitely wasn't the plan, but better late than never.

It was just Bannister, Banks, & Smith when I started with the firm. I like to call those my "pre-Park" days. My life pre-Park included happy hours with the other paralegals, coffee runs with the cute guy in Accounting, and actually getting my coursework done before the sun came up. Then Vanessa had to go and get married and my short-term coverage assignment in Divorce turned into a life sentence working for "Sub Zero".

There are things I like about the man, for sure.

- **He's generous with bonuses.**

I surprised Gabe and Rory with a family trip to Puerto Rico a few years back, all without dipping into my savings.

- **He's incredibly smart.**

Everyone knows he graduated from Yale Law with a 3.9 GPA and was the fastest to complete the partner track in the history of BBS (now BBS&P).

- **He is professional and respectful.**

He never yells at me, or tries to make me look or feel stupid in front of a client.

- **And he's incredibly easy on the eyes.**

The man looks like Keanu Reeves, if Keanu wore impeccable suits 24/7, had sexy horn-rimmed glasses, and spent all his spare time in the gym to get muscles like Brad Pitt in "Fight Club". I've never seen said muscles, but Jennifer in Estate Planning shared an elevator with one of his lady friends and heard the woman mention it while rudely using her cell phone on speaker. Thank God that witch is out of the picture. In addition to being tacky, she often treated me like Henry's personal assistant, instead of a valued member of the legal team.

In truth, there are *more* than a few things I like about Henry Park, Jr. I may even be harboring the *tiniest* crush on the man. It's practically a foregone conclusion with no sexual outlets and a nonexistent social life.

But he's *so* uptight! I wouldn't be surprised if he slept in those fancy suits. And he's obsessed with rules. There's no way someone so rigid could handle a woman with this much *sabor.* And he *never* stops working, not even when he's got a date with one of his many admirers. More than once, I've had to call security on angry women who got past reception and didn't care for being stood up for a date the night before. And worst of all, all of his "lady friends" have been a very specific *type:* tall, *painfully sexy* high-power attorneys, just like him. I bet there's a directory of these women where he can just order one like an Uber.

Henry has a rule against interoffice dating,—*of course* he does—but even if he didn't, I doubt a short Rubenesque paralegal with no Ivy League degree or house in Stamford would fit the bill. *His loss!* I want to live life to the fullest, try everything, and go back for seconds. Hell, maybe even *thirds*. "Brown eyes, thick thighs, and unwilling to compromise" has been my mantra to get over harsh words from terribly unoriginal mean girls in high school and later disgusting taunts from wannabe players in college. I can *certainly* handle a little unrequited crush at work.

Cici clears her throat and gestures to the double doors behind her.

"Mr. Bannister will see you now."

I collect myself and stride purposefully into the founding partner's office, trying not to be intimidated by decor that clearly costs more than a beach house in Nantucket. Mr. Bannister is seated behind his mahogany desk and looking a lot like "Mr. Fantastic", complete with the distinguished gray streaks at his temples. Plenty of the firm's female employees hold a candle for him, hoping to be the next "Mrs. Bannister".

"Good evening, Ms. Sanchez," he says, closing a brief thicker than my tort law textbook. "What brings you by?"

"Hen—I mean *Mr. Park* mentioned you would have names of some potential VIP petitioners? He said you spoke about them at lunch."

Mr. Bannister picks up a manila envelope from his desk and brings it to where I'm standing.

"Their names are Naomi Watanabe and Tanner Moore. You may know Tanner from his fitness empire, TanFit." I take the envelope from Mr. Bannister and peek inside.

"Yes. Mr. Park mentioned he was preparing for an IPO?" Mr. Bannister nods somberly.

"Which means if we get this case, we'll be working in both Eastern and Pacific hours with Mr. Moore's attorney." I use all my willpower to keep from rolling my eyes. Of course the big case when I need to focus on school means even *longer* hours. I paste a professional smile on my face to hide the rage within.

"Thanks, Mr. Bannister. I'm off to put together the client dossiers. Mr. Park is eager to learn about these prospective clients." Mr. Bannister turns back to his desk but stops short.

"Actually, Ms. Sanchez, Mr. Park may know the female petitioner." That gets my attention. I look up to see a ghost of a smile pass across Mr. Bannister's face.

"Really?"

"They were the same year at Yale Law. Hopefully that gives us an edge when it's time to sign the retainer."

"I'm sure it will. Thank you, sir." Mr. Bannister retakes his seat and opens another mammoth brief. *Is it a requirement that all partners dismiss people by just picking back up their work?* I close my legal pad and see myself out. Hopefully Henry knows this Watanabe woman and we get some inside info. If this case means more work, hopefully it also means a fat bonus as my graduation present.

CHAPTER FOUR

Camila

August 10th, 2018

"You're never going to beat him in the office, so don't even try," Vanessa warns, pulling my attention away from her dismal filing system and back to the handoff session she's been half-assing for the last forty-five minutes.

Nothing is ready. Files for active cases are mixed in with files for closed cases. She doesn't have any client numbers saved into her office phone. Her password to the firm intranet—along with all the confidential client files digitally stored there—is on a Post-It note under her keyboard. And her desk has so many knick knacks, there's barely room for the interoffice bin and a single, *completely blank* legal pad. How on earth someone so clearly incompetent earned a spot with a *partner* is beyond me. I can already tell I'll have to re-learn everything from scratch once she's out.

"Sub Zero gets here before 8:00am most days, but as long as I'm in before 8:15am, he doesn't fuss." *Of course* she doesn't even follow the firm's designated hours. If she can get away with it, kudos for her. Meanwhile, I have to elbow my way onto a subway car at 6:30am to get here on time.

I swivel in her chair—*my* chair for the next three weeks—and see her steeling mints from Mark's candy bowl. Hopefully my cube neighbor isn't as much of a ditz as Vanessa seems to be.

"Sub Zero?" I ask. She pauses her plundering to stare at me in disbelief.

"You don't know? Sub Zero is what everyone calls Henry. He's cold as ice. Be glad he's a lawyer, because if he weren't, he'd make an excellent assassin." I cough to cover my giggle.

"Is he really *that* bad?" She leans in close to whisper in my ear.

"He's way worse." She leans back against the cubicle wall and twirls her blonde locks around a pink pen with a feather on the end. "I have to stay late like three days a week because he likes to drop shit on my desk on his way out." I scowl.

"God, I hate that. If you don't want to do it today, neither do I."

"I hear you," she says, giving me a rueful smile. "I know the circumstances aren't great, so thank you again for covering my desk. Sub Zero made a huge stink when I told him I'd be out."

I return her smile, not letting on that I know she didn't give enough notice for her wedding. She's been planning it for over a year—it's all she can talk about at the paralegal happy hours—and still she forgot to let her boss know until three weeks beforehand. I'm the fourth person she had to ask to fill in, and Jonathan pitched a major fit when I agreed to help her. He'll be fine with one of the floaters, considering the Dannemann case just settled.

I open her desk drawer to sneak another look at the mess. *Seriously, how does she find anything in this?* I might stay late tonight so I'm not scrambling tomorrow. Vanessa taps me on the shoulder and jerks her head in the direction of the hallway.

"Look alive." I stand to peek my head over the divider, and my mouth goes dry.

Henry Park, Jr., or Sub Zero as Vanessa insists on calling him, is *gorgeous*. He was only ever a picture on the "Wall of Partners" before now, and it does *not* do him justice.

He's at least 6'2", with shoulders an action star would envy and a jaw that must have been sculpted. Dark brown eyes peer from behind horn-rimmed glasses—my kryptonite—and his mouth is so full and pouty, it's almost obscene. I bet his smile is glorious, though I can already tell he doesn't do it often.. A navy pinstripe suit covers a body likely built by CrossFit, and he moves down the hall with the poise and certainty befitting a newly appointed partner.

His shrewd eyes take in his surroundings before they land on me, freezing me where I stand. Under his piercing gaze, I can't seem to catch my breath. Finally, he comes to stand in front of us, eyebrow raised in interest. He turns to address Vanessa, breaking the spell.

"Hello, Ms. Davies. Did Judge Johnson call during the Russo deposition?" She stops twirling her hair and stands a bit straighter.

"No, Mr. Park." He nods before turning his dazzling eyes in my direction.

"And who is this?"

I've never been a fan of people who talk past a person, and decide to introduce myself. I extend my hand in greeting.

"Hello, sir. My name is Camila Sanchez. I will be your paralegal while Vanessa is out getting married."

He takes my hand to shake it, and I stand firm under his intense scrutiny.

"It's a pleasure to meet you, Ms. Sanchez," he answers, still eyeing me intently. After a thorough once over, his expression relaxes. "I assume Ms. Davies is showing you the ropes?"

That would imply she knows where they are.

"Yes. She's brought me up to speed. I will do my best to provide seamless coverage while she's out."

I flex my fingers nervously and look down to find my hand still in his. He abruptly releases me.

"Very good," he says with all the warmth of a hitman. After a curt nod, he goes into his office, shutting the door behind him and effectively ending the conversation. Suddenly the Sub Zero nickname seems fitting.

Vanessa lets out a breath from beside me.

"See what I mean?! You have been warned. If you want to survive working his desk, make sure you have a thick skin and read this." She pulls a thick, blue binder from the wall-mounted shelf behind me. "Henry created these guidelines for anyone who works with him. If you remember absolutely nothing from our meeting today, but read that binder cover to cover, you will be fine."

"Don't worry, I got this," I assure her. I ignore the doubtful look pulling down the corners of her mouth and pat her on the shoulder.

"I promise. I'll read the binder and follow the rules so you can unplug in the Bahamas knowing I've got everything covered here. Just focus on saying 'I do'." At the mention of her wedding, she beams at me.

"Oh my God. I can't wait. I'm going to come back so tanned, you won't even recognize me." I smile, while inwardly cringing at the thought.

Chapter Five

Henry

Beep! Beep! Beep! Beep!

It's 5:00am. Time to start the day. *Fuck.*

I reach an arm out from under my weighted blanket and blindly feel for the offending alarm. Thanks to custom blackout curtains that cost a pretty penny, it's pitch black in here. Absolute darkness, my weighted blanket, and my noise machine are the only way to guarantee even four hours of uninterrupted sleep, but they do make finding my phone in the morning a bit tricky. I wasn't always a light sleeper; I have memories of my mother furiously cleaning my room around me while I tried in vain to sleep until noon.

But then high school hit and the pressure started. Suddenly tests and essays weren't about grades; they were about qualifying for Honors and AP classes, and laying the foundation for college applications. I won a bitter and long-running argument against my younger (and lesser) twin, Noah, and suddenly I was a legal prodigy, primed to follow in my dad's footsteps as a successful trial attorney, or maybe even a future in politics.

The argument in question? *There's no true altruism because the other person always gets something in return, even if that "something" has no material value.* Noah held onto his Pollyanna outlook for years before I finally convinced him of the fulfillment *he* gets when he finds the perfect gift for mom, or that Dad feels when we ace a test he helped us study for, or the satisfaction Damon (our middle brother) gets when one of his mentees makes the varsity basketball team after attending one of his free clinics at the rec center. There's nothing *wrong* with getting something in return, but it does mean there's no such thing as doing something good just to do it.

When he finally had to admit I was right, Noah looked at me like I'd just told him there's no Santa Claus. I felt terrible for weeks. In hindsight, I'm guessing that's part of why he opted to become an agent rather than going the full lawyer route like Dad and I.

By finals freshman year, Mom had to buy me a mouthguard (I'd started grinding my molars nightly), and I couldn't sleep for more than two hours at a time, if at all. Noah was less than thrilled; we shared a room and my desk light woke him up too some nights. He said my grinding was like nails on a chalkboard. Mom and Dad did all they could do, which was freak out and then send me to a behavioral specialist. Dr. Diaz diagnosed stress and overstimulation pretty quickly and we began our search for therapeutic tools and healthy coping mechanisms.

After years of tweaking, my nightly ritual entails:

- **At least one hour of vigorous physical activity**

Most nights, I knock it out in my home gym. Ever since Cindy Chang invited me over to hang in her hot tub while her parents were out of town sophomore year, the company of a warm and willing woman became an option, too. Few women have been able to match my stamina, however, so I usually still have to take a jog on the treadmill to finish winding down.

- **A cup of warm chamomile tea**

This was sometimes replaced by a hit from a joint during one particularly rebellious summer in college, and later, a nice glass of Merlot once my palette developed. Not *every* night, of course.

- **A long, hot shower** (or bath, if I'm feeling fancy or sore from said *vigorous activity*)

- **A weighted blanket**

- **A noise machine loaded with nature sounds**

- **Blackout curtains** (or a sleep mask, if I'm traveling)

Even with all that, sometimes—like the night before the bar exam, or before the firm announced I made partner—I have to take half a sleeping pill to get my dick of a brain to calm down and let me rest.

If I'm not careful, my backup 5:15am alarm is going to yell at me. I reluctantly push the weighted blanket down and feel for the remote to the curtains; the remote feature was totally worth the extra $2500. Once I can finally see, I grab my phone and make my way to the bathroom.

As I pick up my phone to review my emails and schedule for the day, I look down and realize my "morning friend" is still there, hard and insistent as ever. *Shit.* He's been pretty pissed at me considering the last time he had any feminine company was more than six months ago.

Sorry, pal, but it's not like I can just pull up Tinder. I'm known enough that any relationship (even casual) could potentially impact the firm's reputation. As the P in BBS&P, I'm the face of the company; a scandal from a Tinder hookup gone wrong would be unacceptable. Cory and Adam, my last two brothers, certainly make them seem fun, though. Well, Adam *did*, until he met Maya and decided to burn his little black book. How he could so quickly throw out all the wisdom of his older brothers to get *engaged* of all things, I'll never know, but he seems happy. And Maya is lovely.

Instead of Tinder (or its many copycat apps), I use a service that matches busy, high-profile professionals seeking discreet hookups. It's actually still a lot like Tinder, since members need to match to meet, but the screening process was a bitch, I needed a referral to join, and the quarterly membership fee has a comma in it. I even have to send in clean STD results every quarter. The whole thing was a bit invasive when I first joined (at the request of Sean Smith, one of the other partners), but you can't argue with the results.

Unfortunately, BBS&P has been even busier than normal this year. Love and marriage are the foolish fantasies of children. They're not worth surrendering half your assets in the event of a divorce, and yet everyone keeps fucking getting married. I shouldn't complain,—it's guaranteed job security—but lately there haven't been enough hours in the day to read through all the client files and prep for court, let alone have sex. I doubt anyone at work can tell, but I feel like a volcano about to erupt most days.

I sigh, resigned to having to take myself in hand *again*. I may be closer to forty than twenty, but I'm still a healthy man with a *very* healthy sex drive. This is barely going to scratch the surface. It's time I finally cashed in some vacation and had a good, old fashioned fuck fest somewhere tropical so I can take the edge off and refocus on work. Maybe after they announce the top earners for this year...

I walk back to my bedroom and sit sideways on my bed, my legs hanging off the side. Without even having to look, I reach in my bedside table drawer for the lube and the stretchy silicon toy. I tug the waistband of my pajamas down, squeeze a few drops of lube into the toy, and push the mouth end down on my dick.

I squeeze and stroke the toy up and down with practiced efficiency, getting the job done in less than five minutes. It barely even raises my heart rate. I look down at the creamy spatter on my pajama bottoms and frown. Call me a romantic, but I'd much prefer a *person* attached to a mouth on my dick. I grab a tissue (also without looking) and wipe off most of my release before dropping it into the wastebasket and my pajamas into the hamper. *Yes, I am truly living the dream.*

Ding!

I just got an email but...where is my phone? It's not on the bedside table. It sounded far away...I continue my search for the misplaced device, trying to retrace my steps before remembering I left my phone next to the sink. I jog back to the bathroom to retrieve the message, my now soft member slapping lightly against my thigh. Given the time, it's probably the VIP client profiles I had Ms. Sanchez put together. I see her name on the lock screen and smile; *that's my girl.*

As I open the file, however, my smile immediately drops. *What the fuck?! Naomi Watanabe? Fucking Naomi Watanabe from Yale Law? My childish heartbreak come to taunt me at my place of business all these years later?*

I sink down on the closed lid of the commode and scroll through the file, my jaw slack in disbelief. *She fucking* married *Tanner? That guy was the king of douchebags!* Sure, he hit it big with some fitness craze (something to do with rowing), but based on his complete lack of character and history, I'd bet he *stole* that idea. He was certainly a fan of stealing in grad school.

If Naomi actually *married* Tanner, I definitely dodged a bullet all those years ago. I clearly didn't know her at all.

I throw the phone through the bathroom door to land on my bed. I'll finish reading through the dossiers on the drive in; luckily I have my own background information on these clients. I breathe in through my nose and out through my mouth to quiet the rage itching under my skin. I stomp into my walk-in closet and pull out a suit, shirt, tie, cufflinks, and the most expensive shoes I own. *I'm a professional. I can handle representing my sort-of ex in a divorce against my former teammate and mortal enemy.* But I will look so fucking good it hurts when I do. *Eat your heart out, Naomi.*

On the ride in, I discover that Naomi and Tanner actually got married right after graduation. Apparently the announcement was within months of the couple announcing they were expecting. *Can anyone say shotgun wedding?* Together, they share a nine-year-old daughter who made the move to NYC with Naomi. It sucks that there's a kid involved; the kids almost always lose when it comes to divorce.

Mediations as part of a separation agreement broke down quickly; either Tanner was a no-show, claiming some conflict related to his IPO, or they devolved into screaming matches. Almost at the office, I scroll through the file again to see the details on Naomi's successful environmental law practice. She looked to be just months away from making partner. I can't believe she would walk away from all that. Looking at her case records, she's clearly fierce and formidable, but New York is cutthroat. She'll have her work cut out for her starting over at a new firm.

There's information about Tanner and Naomi's board seats, memberships, global real estate holdings, and even about their daughter's former private school. All that's missing is the financial information, which we won't be able to get until the retainer is signed. The dossiers are beyond comprehensive; Ms. Sanchez clearly deserves a bonus.

I exit the car in the underground garage and ride the elevator up in silence. *Do I mention my connection with Naomi?* Law school was ages ago, but I *was* practically in love with her. But it was before I was even a lawyer, and we were never officially *together*. I'd say this is ethically light gray at best. Bill likely assumed I'd be the best fit since we were at Yale at the same time. He's not wrong; I do bring another level of understanding for this client. *Or maybe I don't.* Naomi *now* might be nothing like Naomi *then*; I'm certainly not the same person I was back then.

It's settled. There is no reasonable conflict of interest. *I will work with Naomi like any other client because I'm a goddamn professional.*

Ding!

Too soon, the elevator doors open onto my floor and I make my way to my corner office, doing my best to avoid the trail of sweat making its way down my spine. Is the AC not working today? *Get it together, Henry!*

"Good morning, Mr. Park," Ms. Sanchez practically sings. *At least* someone's *in a good mood today.*

"Ms. Sanchez," I nod, before heading into my office and closing the door. Two minutes later she comes in, trusty legal pad in hand. She's looking at me too shrewdly, and I clear my throat.

"Thank you for the excellent work you did in putting together those client backgrounds, Ms. Sanchez. They were beyond thorough." She smiles and pink colors her cheeks.

"Thank you, Mr. Park. Ms. Watanabe is already seated in Conference Room A. Will you be meeting her directly or connecting with Mr. Bannister first?"

Greeting Nao—*Ms. Watanabe* on my own may give us the opportunity to diffuse any awkwardness, but it might also increase the impression of impropriety given our previous relationship. Better to walk in as a united front with Bill.

"I'll stop by Mr. Bannister's so we can meet Ms. Watanabe together."

"Very good." Ms. Sanchez is still looking at me too closely. She opens her mouth as if about to say something, but closes it just as quickly. With three quick taps of her pen on her legal pad, she exits my office, closing the door behind her.

CHAPTER SIX

Henry

December 15th, 2020

"So," Ms. Sanchez says, her hip propped against my desk as usual, clicking her ever present pen. "Are you and the family celebrating Christmas together this year, or are you going to play it safe?"

Governor Cuomo cleared law firms to resume in-person operations in June, and the entire office has been working in shifts for the last six months to avoid triggering a super spreader event. Everyone has to wear masks, there's a disinfecting station on every floor, and luckily, we've only had eight mild cases since coming back. Things have been *different*, but at this point, they're manageable.

No one expected a Hallmark Christmas after a year of hell, but that all changed once the vaccine went public. Now, there's hope in the air, mixed with a fair amount of nerves. Some of the partners already managed to get the shot, but most people still have to rely on masks and rubbing alcohol.

"We're going to play it safe. Mom and Dad aren't on the priority list for the vaccine, and Damon's paranoid he won't be able to play ball if he gets sick."

Ms. Sanchez grins before bending down to retrieve something from behind the couch in my office. She's got on a knee-length wool skirt in dark gray, a plain white dress shirt, and a cardigan covered in reindeer and snowmen. The monstrosity was lit up with real Christmas lights when she first came in, but I had her turn them off so they wouldn't be a distraction.

Looking at her bent over, I'm distracted for an entirely different reason now. My eyes catch on the delicate line of her ankles, the smooth expanse of her calves, and up to her thick thighs before they disappear under the festive ensemble. Lately, I've been noticing Ms. Sanchez for reasons beyond the professional, and it's a problem. I clear my throat, along with the surprisingly lustful thoughts that threaten to overwhelm me.

Ms. Sanchez finally ends my torture, coming from behind the couch with a gift basket almost half her size. She laughs at my dumbfounded expression.

"Relax. It's not really for you. Most productions are still shut down, so Rory's been making care packages for anyone who can't celebrate together. I grabbed one for you just in case. You can drop it by your parents' or something." She lugs the basket to my desk and sets it down with a heavy thump.

"Wow," I say, because there are no words. Inside the package, there are two mugs full of instant hot cocoa and cider packets, candy canes in assorted colors, brightly wrapped chocolates in the shape of Christmas trees and wreaths, a small artificial poinsettia, a tube of ten ornaments, a string of jingle bells, and a headband with reindeer antlers. Everything sits on a bed of holly and ivy garland.

At my silence, Ms. Sanchez's smile wilts at the edges.

"I know she went a little overboard. My family goes all out for Christmas and she just thought, especially this year, people could use a little extra cheer. You don't have to—" I put my hand on hers, stopping her rambling. Her skin is warm and velvet soft.

"It's very thoughtful, Ms. Sanchez. Thank you." She gives me a tentative smile and her hand twitches, reminding me to move mine away.

"You're welcome," she says, her voice breathless.

The air in my office suddenly feels thick with possibility. I lean back to put more distance between us.

"What about you? Are you and your family spending the holiday together?" She shakes her head, her expression sad.

"Rory doesn't want to risk it in case she gets a call that production has restarted, and Gabe said he and his roommates are going to do something since we're not doing the family thing. It'll just be me, 'A Christmas Story', and my own special gift basket from Rory." She leans forward and winks. "Mine has alcohol." I quirk my lips.

"Keeping the good stuff for yourself, I see."

"I *did* have to carry three of those baskets all the way from the Bronx. I think I deserve the hard stuff." I ignore the naughty connotation of her words.

"I think everyone does."

She laughs and turns to leave.

"Ms. Sanchez?" I call after her. She looks back at me. "Merry Christmas."

CHAPTER SEVEN

Camila

Present Day

I can tell something's off with Henry. He usually replies back right away with questions on the dossiers, often calling me to confirm details and ask clarifying questions that sometimes lead to pivotal insights into the client. Today, it's been radio silence. If not for the much appreciated kudos this morning,—which I more than earned, since I was stuck at the office until almost eleven—I wouldn't know he even received the completed files. He also looks surprisingly clammy and hot for someone who goes by Sub Zero. Maybe he's coming down with something.

I reach the door to the conference room just as he and Mr. Bannister arrive, still discussing the details from the dossiers. He lifts his shoulders in a barely perceptible shrug to ease the tension in his obviously stiff shoulders (also unusual) and presses his lips into a grim line before smoothing his face into its usual placid facade. *What is going on with him today?*

There's a question in my eyes which Henry avoids by averting his gaze and pulling open the door to the conference room. I suppress a sigh and follow him into the room, taking my usual seat in the row of chairs along the wall. *Someday I'll get a seat at the table. Just one more mid-term and then the hellacious bar prep begins.*

Ms. Watanabe is seated directly across from Mr. Bannister and she is a vision. Hair as smooth and dark as ebony cascades to the middle of her back. Some uber-professional women opt to downplay their femininity, but she's emphasizing hers, showing a hint of cleavage in a fitted burgundy dress with cap sleeves that reveal her svelte form. Her eyes are captivating, like Mulan in the animated movie. *Shit. That's probably racist, but it's also accurate.* Her eyes are almost *too* big, which would be enough to make her beautiful, but her full lips in a matching burgundy shade make her striking. Looking at her makes me question whether I've been too closed off by only dating men. It also makes me wish I bought more than frozen yogurt and a cardigan on my last trip to Bloomingdale's.

Those too-big eyes widen slightly when they come to rest on Henry and I notice him shift in his chair from my seat behind him. Something is *definitely* up. Do they know each other? She *is* exactly the type of woman he tends to go for: stunning and unapproachably attractive.

After the initial awkwardness, the meeting proceeds as normal. Ms. Watanabe is as impressive as she looks, and just joined our biggest competitor in the environmental division. Maybe she can finally crack the mystery of why NYC water seems to almost bubble right out of the tap. It certainly does make a good bagel, though. In a decision that surprises no one, she signs the retainer agreement before the meeting is even done; BBS&P *is* the best, after all. Mr. Bannister is beyond thrilled, practically fawning all over her and insisting he treat her to a celebratory breakfast at Buvette.

The three of them collect their designer briefcases, straighten their designer clothes, and head towards the elevators for a chic breakfast billable at $1700 an hour between the two partners. I sigh wistfully at my live viewing of "Lifestyles of the Rich & Famous: Corporate Edition" and head back to eat my tuna sandwich at my desk. When he's back, I definitely plan on grilling Henry about what really happened in this meeting.

Henry's not back from breakfast until almost noon, which has given me enough time to brainstorm no less than five scenarios for his weird behavior this morning.

- Option 1: He's been body-snatched, and we are in the early stages of "Soylent Green".

- Option 2: He had a wild night last night with one too many Earl Greys and he's "hung over".

- Option 3: He and Ms. Watanabe used to press their equally sexy bodies together on a regular basis.

- Option 4: Ms. Watanabe used to date one of his brothers and he's got a bitter grudge for the heartbreak she obviously left in her wake.

- Option 5: Something is going on with his family that's too bad for even him to bottle up.

As he passes me on the way into his office, I notice his tie is a bit loose and he's even got the top button of his shirt unbuttoned. *What?!* Option 6: He just tried *crack* for the first time because that's the only way he'd come even close to a dress code violation. He doesn't even notice when I follow him in before he can close the door behind him. He simply sinks into his chair and stares off to a spot behind me, deep in thought. *OK. Time for an intervention.*

I clear my throat to get his attention.

"Sir?"

His eyes focus on me like he just realized I was in the room, and he sits up straighter in his chair.

"Ms. Sanchez. I didn't see you there. How may I help you?"

I click my pen nervously before taking a breath and steeling myself against a potential chastisement for discussing something personal at work.

"Sir..." I lick my lips nervously and start again. "Sir, are you...OK?"

He lifts his eyebrows and presses his lips into another frown.

"What do you mean, Ms. Sanchez?"

I will myself to stop clicking my pen and take another calming breath.

"This morning, at the meeting with Ms. Watanabe, you didn't seem...yourself."

He continues to frown at me, but says nothing. Just like a lawyer to stay silent, giving me the opportunity to dig my own grave by babbling to fill the silence.

"You seemed a bit nervous right before the meeting, which is unusual. And she didn't say anything, but I could swear Ms. Watanabe recognized you when you came in. And now you're back from breakfast and your tie..."

I let the sentence dangle, worried I've already earned some sort of demerit for daring to question a partner. After a tense silence, he sighs and moves to button his shirt and fix his tie. *Damn. I was kinda enjoying Disheveled Henry.*

"Very astute, Ms. Sanchez, as always."

His tie and shirt back in position, he's now Sub Zero once more. *Great.* I've clearly pissed him off.

"You are right that Ms Watanabe and I know each other. We had a brief and very minor personal relationship during law school which I disclosed to Mr. Bannister this morning before the meeting. I assured him that it would not impact my representation of Ms. Watanabe. Do I need to make the same assurance to you?"

His eyebrow lifts and his eyes harden. I clearly crossed the line; Sub Zero is now Arctic Blast. I try to ignore the strict daddy vibes he's giving off that have me tingling between my legs. I don't normally play the submissive, but I'd definitely make an exception for Henry.

"My apologies, sir. I meant no offense."

With a small nod of acceptance and a click of his mouse, I'm dismissed. I scurry out of his office, closing the door behind me. *How badly did I just fuck up? Do I need to start looking at openings on LinkedIn?* Rather than obsess, I drop my notepad at my desk before retreating to the kitchen for some carby comfort; there's gotta be some leftover bagels or a muffin or *something*.

Jonathan, my old boss, is there as well, raiding the cupcakes from a birthday celebration earlier in the day. *Jackpot.* He raises his red velvet in greeting.

"Hi Camila. How's Sub Zero treating you? Still making your life miserable on a daily basis?"

I hide my wince by biting into my chosen German chocolate cupcake. God, I wish he wasn't right. Ever since I left to cover Henry's desk and never came back, Jonathan has been a sore loser. We're in the same department, but instead of collaborating, Jonathan's holding a grudge for daring to advance my career. He was a *fine* boss, but who would pass up the opportunity (and significant pay bump) to support a partner? Of course, it doesn't help that Henry isn't afraid to keep all the best clients for himself.

"I'm doing well, Jonathan. Thank you for asking."

He grunts sullenly into his cupcake.

"I heard you got another VIP client. What's that, like the fourth this year?"

I mentally count and fight to keep the smile off my lips.

"The fifth, actually." Jonathan's mouth tightens.

"Congratulations," he says, his voice dripping with sarcasm. "If only we could *all* skip paying our dues and go right to the big leagues."

When I only blink in response, Jonathan stalks back to his office, looking more like a pouty toddler than an attorney. What a tool. He can be mad about my promotion all he wants, but if I couldn't hang, Henry would not have kept me.

"Does he often antagonize you in the office?"

I nearly jump out of my kitten heels at Henry's voice behind me. He must have snuck in for coffee during my standoff with Jonathan. I give a noncommittal lift of one shoulder.

"Nothing I can't handle." A true Bronx girl like myself can handle bullies (even of the corporate variety) without breaking a sweat.

He watches me intently, looking like he might say something. Instead, he turns back to add creamer to his mug. If this day could go ahead and wrap it up, that would be great.

"And that was it? He just gave you the silent treatment for the rest of the day?"

Rory downs the last of her amaretto sour and motions to the bartender for a refill. When Henry let me out before 6:00pm for the first time in *literally ever*, I knew drinks with my sister were in order. She recommended we check out this dive bar in Brooklyn known for their strong drinks and Southern-themed cuisine. I swirl around the ice clumping at the bottom of my piña colada and try not to think about my nightmare commute back home later. *Not everyone lives in Williamsburg now, Rory.*

"Basically. I took dictation for a brief in the afternoon, but he was in his office with the door closed otherwise."

She rolls her eyes.

"With a stick that big up his ass, how does he even shit? Like, does he need to see a doctor once a month for relief, or..."

I snort, spilling some of my drink down my blouse. My kid sis certainly has a way with words.

"Oh my God, Rory! I did *not* need that image in my head."

Rory's smile turns wicked.

"What image? The image of your boss, bent over his $4,000 desk, his tie flung over his shoulders and his Hugo Boss slacks around his ankles, getting the rubber glove treatment from some brawny nurse named Bruno?"

I can't help it; I spit my drink down my blouse, half laugh-ing-half coughing as I try to recover.

"Are you trying to kill me?" Rory just takes a sip of her drink, like her comment didn't just destroy me. "I'd actually pay good money to see that. I'd pay extra if they skipped the lube."

At that, my sister raises an eyebrow. *What? He's my boss, but I'm not allowed to make fun of him?*

"What, pray tell, would my older sister, Patron Saint of Workaholics and Granny Panty Fan Club President, know about *lube*?"

Oh, I see. I'm allowed to make fun of my boss, but, through some cosmic joke, my sister thinks I'm a prude. I haven't exactly had a ton of spare time. I hide my hurt at the jab by blotting my now damp shirt.

"Hey! I get out! I have Tinder and Bumble on my phone right now." My sister smirks, clearly not believing me. It *has* been a while... "And, in defense of granny panties, they are both comfortable and cheap for a girl on a budget."

"Ah yes. Affordability and comfort; the path to every man's heart."

I roll my eyes at my sister—she's sassier than Rosie Perez and Marisa Tomei combined—and stand up from our booth.

"Thanks to you, I've got about half a cup of ice sloshing around in my bra. I'll be right back. Order me another one when the waiter comes back?"

Her smile says she knows I'm dodging the topic of my sex life,—or lack thereof—but she just nods. I make my way through the crowded bar, edging between harried servers and tipsy hipsters on my way to the restroom. The crowd here is a little on the young side, mostly in their early 20s. At thirty, I feel a bit like an undercover cop from 21 Jump Street. Just when I'm almost past the overcrowded bar area, a group of women clearly out for a bachelorette party nearly knock me over. *They're not going to run out of alcohol people! No need to push and shove.*

I make myself as small as possible with curves like mine and continue to inch through the crowd. And that's when I see him...Or...*Them*? Sitting in the booth right next to the bathrooms is Henry, Jr. and another man who looks nearly identical, minus the glasses and with a way flashier suit. Am I being punked? I knew he had brothers, but a twin? Apparently I stare a little too hard and "Flashy Suit Henry" makes eye contact with me and smiles. *Busted.*

"Care to join us, beautiful?"

"Flashy Suit Henry"'s smile is warm and welcoming. My eyes dart to Henry; his hair is sticking out in several directions like he's been raking his hands through it, his shirt and tie are loose,—twice in one day?!—and his eyes have a slight droop from a few too many cocktails. He doesn't seem bothered by his brother's invitation, or by my seeing him looking unkempt once again.

"Don't worry about Mr. Stuffy Pants here," he gestures to Henry, who lets out an ungentlemanly snort into his drink. "When he pointed you out, I knew I just had to meet the woman he spends practically every waking moment with."

I bite my lower lip and glance at my table. Rory is watching us closely.

"Uh...I don't want to impose...And I'm here with my sister."

"Bring her over, too," offers "Flashy Suit Henry". "I just landed a client and I need to celebrate. And you, of all people, know that Henry could use a few drinks." Another snort from Henry.

"Are you buying?"

"Flashy Suit Henry" looks at me like I'm crazy.

"Of course! We're not barbarians."

I press my lips together to hide a smile. Apparently, this twin got all the charm. I motion Rory to come over and turn towards the bathroom.

"I've got to use the facilities, but my little sister, Rory," I point to her as she makes her way through the crowd, "is on her way over. Please wait until I'm back to tell any embarrassing stories about my boss."

"Flashy Suit Henry" chuckles.

"You got it."

CHAPTER EIGHT

Camila

On my way down the hall from the restroom, I brace myself for an uncomfortable night of forced laughs and awkward small talk with the gorgeous man who holds my future in his hands, and his equally hot twin. Henry gets 8am to 7pm most days and now he wants my first night out in months too?

I scan the bar, hoping for a possible escape route. Rory won't have any trouble keeping them entertained. Anyway, it's not like she hasn't ditched *me* at a club before, usually to hook up with a hot bartender or bouncer. The tipsy hipsters are chugging Pabst Blue Ribbon at the bar, and the women from the bachelorette party settled in the booth Rory and I were in. They seem to be trying to drown out the rest of the room with their shrieks and laughter; I can only imagine the headache I'd get if I sat anywhere near them.

I finally risk a glance at the booth with my boss, and see Rory with her head tilted back in a full-on laugh. She's almost tearing up! *What the hell?* I push my way to the table and her eyes widen when she sees me.

"Mila! Oh my God! How come you never told me your boss is so funny?"

Maybe because five minutes ago, I wouldn't have thought Mr. Uptight even knew what a joke was? Instead of answering her, I do my best impression of a fish gasping for air.

"Uh..."

Henry gives me a sardonic grin.

"Unfortunately, she wouldn't know. There's hardly an opportunity for jokes when we're validating allegations of infidelity and negotiating alimony payments large enough to buy a condo in Greenwich, is there, Mila?"

I slide into the booth next to Rory, still gaping at "Bizarro Henry" and trying to ignore the tingle I got when he called me Mila.

"Um, yeah...Definitely."

I choose to ignore Henry's raised eyebrow at my lack of eloquence and extend my hand to "Flashy Suit Henry" instead. I give him my most charming smile. Henry's jaw clenches.

"I'm Camila Sanchez. It's great to meet you."

"Oh, how rude of me!" he says, pumping my outstretched hand enthusiastically. "I'm Noah, Henry's more stylish, more handsome, and definitely more fun, younger brother."

Henry rolls his eyes and elbows Noah in the ribcage.

"You're only younger by six minutes."

"It still counts, bro," Noah replies, rubbing the pain out of his side.

I laugh lightly at the brotherly teasing, even though I still can't get over that I'm now seeing *two* jacked Keanus, and the one I've been secretly fantasizing about for years has suddenly grown a sense of humor. *I will not fuck my boss. I will not fuck my boss.* The veins in his hands as he fingers the rim of his whiskey glass catch my eye and I gulp. *I might fuck my boss. Or at least try.*

I clear my throat, supercharged images now swirling around in my head.

"It's a pleasure to meet you, Noah."

I take a sip of my refilled piña colada (*Thanks, Rory!*) and feel my composure returning.

"So, what brings you both to Brooklyn? I know Henry lives in Westchester, so..."

"Like I said earlier, I'm here to celebrate. My company was just chosen to handle the US representation for Song Kang. He's—"

"From 'Forecasting Love and Weather'?!," I practically screech. Rory winces and Henry and Noah exchange shocked glances.

"You know that show?" asks Noah.

"No. I don't *know* that show. I *love* that show! Song Kang is super hot." My cheeks redden and Noah doesn't try to hide his grin.

"Forgive my sister," Rory interrupts before I can continue my ode to all things Song Kang. "Mila is *obsessed* with K-dramas. She knows all the actors. She has a watch party any time a new show drops." Rory continues, despite the scarlet shade of my cheeks. "She even taught herself how to make chamchi gimbap and hoedeopbap. My brother, Gabe, and I were her guinea pigs. Did I say that right?"

"You sure did," Noah smiles, clearly amused and surprised by my fan-girling. *Dios mío! Why couldn't I keep my mouth shut?* I can feel the redness spreading down to my neck.

"What can I say?" I shrug. "The food in all of them looks so good, I just had to try it. If this one," I point to Henry, "ever lets me take a vacation, I might have to visit Seoul in person."

"If you want authentic Korean food without the expensive flight, you can always come to our house on Sundays. With five sons who were like bottomless pits, Mom can throw down."

My eyes dart back to Henry to gauge his reaction to the invitation; he's bobbing his head in agreement. *Can a person die from shock?*

"Sure. I'll have to take you up on that." *Not.*

For the next hour, the drinks keep flowing and Noah wows us all with stories of crazy clients. He doesn't give us names, of course, but from what I can tell, all actors are either crazy, neurotic, high-maintenance, or all three. If Entertainment Law is in my future, at least it won't be boring.

Henry tells a few embarrassing stories at Noah's expense, but avoids anything about clients, even without sharing names. Ever the boy scout. Meanwhile, I've been plotting Rory's death for flirting so shamelessly, falling all over him whenever he says something even remotely clever. She and I are going to have to have some *serious* girl talk later.

Despite doing his best to maintain the celebratory mood, something still seems off with Henry. His smiles don't reach his eyes, and I'm guessing whatever was bothering him at work is still in the back of his head. Noah stands from the table, gulping down the last of his whiskey soda.

"All right, ladies and gents. I've got to call it a night."

"Boo!," yells Rory, eager to continue the party. Ah, to be twenty-five again. Noah lets out a good-natured chuckle.

"Sorry to kill the party, Rory." He eats a fry off Henry's plate. "As I said, I've got the tab. Get home safely, everyone."

Rory stands up and grabs her cardigan. It may be spring, but winter isn't quite ready to let go.

"I need to head out, too. I'm doing some AD work for my friend's indie production and I'm pretty sure call time is," she looks at her watch and groans, "five hours from now."

"Ouch!" says Henry. He stands to hug Rory as she leaves. "Nice to meet you, Rory. Get home safe."

She hugs him back tightly, and I have to suppress a growl. I avert my eyes to hide my jealousy, but when I look up, she winks and walks towards the door. *Busted again!* Noah looks meaningfully between Henry and I.

"Looks like it's just you two. Don't do anything I wouldn't do."

Henry rolls his eyes and settles back down in his seat.

"Later, bro."

And now we're alone. It's just me, my super hot boss, and way too many drinks. I'm pretty sure there are at least ten movies about this sort of thing. Henry's leaned back against the back of the booth, his eyes closed. His Adam's apple is pronounced against his strong and defined neck. *Am I really checking out a neck? Get a grip, girl!* I clear my throat, hoping that will clear my lustful thoughts, too.

"So, are you drunk enough to tell me the truth about you and our new VIP client?" Henry lifts his head and opens his mouth to protest. "And don't tell me it's nothing, because you were *not* yourself today."

He sighs and actually seems a bit chagrined. I've never seen the expression on his face, and it makes him look ten years younger. Vulnerable.

"Well..." he hesitates briefly, before shrugging to himself and continuing. "Naomi wasn't technically my girlfriend, but we knew each other in the biblical sense during law school. Right before I was going to take things to the next level, she hooked up with my teammate from crew."

Henry can tell from my face, I don't know what "crew" is.

"That's rowing? The long, skinny boats with four guys on them?"

"Got it. Continue."

Henry looks confused.

"There's not much more to the story. Apparently, she liked my teammate enough to marry him. He's Tanner Moore, fitness mogul and her soon-to-be ex-husband."

I sit back against the booth, flabbergasted.

"Shit. What are the odds?"

"Indeed."

"But," I lean forward and look Henry in the eye. "I don't get it. So she's an old hookup. The world is small. Why did that have you sweating in the meeting this morning?"

Henry frowns, looking like a petulant middle schooler.

"I was *not* sweating."

I giggle. I can't help but want to poke the bear.

"You were too. And then you came back from lunch looking like you'd slept in your clothes. Thank goodness you stayed holed up in your office."

I laugh at how uncomfortable Henry looks.

"Well..." He downs his Black Label and clears his throat. "First, let me say thank you for not pointing all that out while we were in the office."

"Of course. I would never do anything to jeopardize your standing at work."

"Second, you're right. I guess you could call Naomi my," he looks *really* uncomfortable now, but something tells me it's the wrong time to laugh, "first love. At least...I loved *her*. She broke my dumb, twenty-four-year-old heart, but she never even knew I felt that way about her." As if realizing he's revealed too much, he straightens. "But again, it will not stop me from doing my job to the best of my ability. It was forever ago. And I'm a professional."

I give him my best "understanding" face, usually reserved for when one of Gabriel's unrequited crushes shot him down, or when Aurora slashed her ex's tires when he dumped her right before taking a semester abroad. *Gosh, they are full-on* adults *now.*

"Henry, don't worry about it. I know you wouldn't let some history get in the way of helping a client. You're the best attorney I know, and still you have morals and character. I don't know if you realize how rare that is."

He smiles, his thigh brushing mine under the table.

"Thank you, Camila. That actually means a lot to me."

I gasp, and Henry pulls his leg back, alarmed.

"What's wrong?"

"It's just...you called me 'Camila'."

He looked confused.

"That's your name, isn't it?"

"Yeah, but you *never* call me that. It's *always* 'Ms. Sanchez'."

Henry relaxes and lets his knee once again bump mine.

"I am a bit uptight, aren't I?"

I laugh weakly, unsure whether I should agree in case he remembers this on Monday.

"You said it, not me."

He laughs and scoots even closer so our entire sides are pressed together. My skin feels like it's on fire and goosebumps break out all over my body.

"That's just at the office. There's no reason I can't call you by your name when we're on our own. Camila is a beautiful name, by the way."

He's leaning even closer now, stroking his hand lightly up and down my arm. I shrugged out of my suit jacket as soon as we got here, and my arms are bare to him in just my silk shell.

He's staring at my mouth now. Either Henry is about to kiss me, or I'm experiencing the first signs of a stroke. He leans in, slow enough to give me the chance to retreat, should I choose. But I wouldn't. Not with how I feel tonight. Not after all these years.

Tonight, I release a contented sigh as he presses his lips against mine. The kiss is delicate at first, restrained because neither of us know whether we should cross this line. I open my mouth in invitation, and that's all he needs to slip his tongue inside.

And now I see why all those women embarrassed themselves for another date. He is a *god* with his mouth. His tongue expertly strokes against mine, his lips firm and insistent. He puts one hand around my throat and the other at my nape to tilt my head and deepen the kiss. *I see you, Mr. Park! Who knew you had kissing game like this?!*

I can do nothing but grab hold of his sides while he plunders my mouth. My panties are a lost cause at this point; someone decided to replace my pussy with Niagara Falls. But eventually, my brain recovers and I remember that I've got kissing skills, too.

I pull his hands from my neck and place them on my hips, before hugging him close and taking over the kiss. He moans in approval as my hands run up and down his back, even using my nails at some points. I let one hand venture to the front of his pants and discover that someone has replaced Henry's dick with the Eiffel Tower—it's hard as steel and sticking straight up. Thank God the booth offers us some privacy.

I kiss him with all the longing I've felt for him, all the pent up sexual tension I thought only I could feel. We pass dominance back and forth between us like a volleyball, the kiss so intense that I don't notice his hand has moved until it's squeezing my right breast.

"Holy shit, Henry!"

He smiles against my lips before going back to unraveling me, his thumb brushing my nipple while the other hand squeezes my hip.

98.7% of my brain is totally on board with this. Henry is hot, he's built, and, from what I just felt, he's packing. If his mouth can do wizardry, I am more than down to find out what his *dick* can do.

But that pesky 1.3% keeps whispering, *What's going to happen on Monday? Is it a good idea to get involved when you know it can't go anywhere because of all his stupid rules? Could you be his paralegal and his secret hookup and still hold on to your dignity?*

And it fucking sucks, because I'm pretty sure that 1.3% is right. I start to slow the kiss, and gently ease away.

"As much fun as this is," Henry smirks and God! it looks hot on him, "it's getting pretty late and I've got to get home to the Bronx. Hopefully the trains are still running."

That's a complete lie. Nothing's waiting for me at home but that mid-term I still need to take. I just know that if he keeps kissing me like that, I'm going to fuck him; damn the consequences!

Henry smiles, his lips looking deliciously swollen from our kiss. I take a mental picture.

"It *is* getting a bit late." Damn, he didn't put up much of a fight. "But if you think I'm letting you take the subway home at this hour, you don't know me at all."

He stands up from the booth, grabs his jacket and offers me his hand.

"C'mon. I'll have Murray drive you home."

"But what about you?" Because no way are we riding together. I don't think I'd be able to restrain myself in a car with him all the way to the Bronx. He shrugs, unbothered by the idea of stranding himself in Brooklyn.

"My parents live not too far from here. I'll just crash there tonight and have Murray pick me up in the morning."

"OK," I say, suddenly shy. How do you say "good night" after a kiss like that?

We step into the cool night air, and a black Escalade pulls up to the curb. Henry opens the door for me and helps me into the car, his hand warm on mine.

"Good night, Camila. Get home safely."

His voice is a purr, and now all I want to do is pet him.

"You too, Henry."

He smiles, steps back, and closes the heavy door, extinguishing the current sparking between us. My address is already entered into the GPS, and Murray wordlessly begins navigating the narrow Brooklyn streets.

Shit. What just happened?

CHAPTER NINE

Henry

This is what death feels like. I'm certain of it. The tiny jackhammer in my head pairs beautifully with the rusty nails piercing my eyeballs every time a ray of sunlight manages to get past my sleep mask. I untangle my arm from the practically vintage flannel sheets on my childhood bed, but when I reach to pull down my mask, I'm met with more face instead. *Huh.*

Keeping my eyes firmly closed, I feel under my pillow for my sleep mask, and...nothing. *Double huh.*

I fumble for my glasses on the bedside dresser and proceed to knock off several AP textbooks and an ancient package of Pop Tarts in the process. *Way to turn my room into a time capsule, Mom.*

No longer blind but still heavily incapacitated, I sneak a peak from under my eyelids to see the culprit behind the rusty nails: my curtains are wide open, letting in the springtime sun, the chirping of birds, and the sound of cyclists whizzing by Mom and Dad's Clinton Hill brownstone.

I slept through the night with no sleep mask or blackout curtains and no noise machine? I tug on my sheets to check. Yep. Unweighted. And I'm in yesterday's clothes, so I definitely didn't have a shower. *How much alcohol did I drink last night that I didn't need the sleep ritual I've used for 20+ years?* From the feel of the jackhammer in my head, I'm guessing *all of it.*

"Henry, Jr.!! Did you want any breakfast before you head back?!" Mom yells from downstairs, replacing the jackhammer in my head with ice picks. Seconds too late, I wrap my pillow around my ears, desperate to escape the noise.

"Marie!" Dad's deep baritone answers, splitting my head open like a ripe melon. "Leave him be. He's clearly sleeping off a bender."

OK. That's enough. I pull myself out of bed, the pillow still tightly wrapped around my ears, and practically slither downstairs, holding onto the railing for dear life. I find my parents in the kitchen. Dad has his arms wrapped around Mom from behind as she stirs scrambled eggs on the stove. I flop onto the barstool at the counter.

"Why were you two yelling if you're in the same room together?" I whisper around a mouth full of sand.

Both my parents turn and level me with a look that makes it clear they knew what they were doing. I take my pillow from around my ears and lay it on the counter, followed by my throbbing head. *So Mom and Dad have jokes. I see how it is.*

"So, do you want any breakfast, Junior?" Mom asks in her perpetually cheery voice. "I'm making eggs, and bacon is already done."

The corner of Dad's mouth twitches.

"Perhaps some 'hair of the dog'?"

I sigh and prop myself up on one fist.

"Yes to the eggs and bacon and no to 'hair of the dog'. I might need to take a break from the hard stuff for the next few months. Maybe years."

Dad chuckles and hands me a cup of coffee. I smile gratefully.

"What had you out partying like a college kid? I don't think I've ever seen you hung over."

"That's because this is a first for me." I gulp down some of the black gold and almost moan when it dampens the booming in my head. "And a *last*. I was out celebrating a new client with Noah."

Mom turns to get flour and sugar from the cabinet for what looks like pancakes. *Sweet!* If crashing at home means a spread like this, I may have to make it a habit.

"Oh! Who did he sign?"

"Some K-drama heart throb. Camila went crazy over him." I tried and failed to keep the edge out of my voice.

Mom drops her whisk abruptly and turns to face me. The smile on her faces stretches from ear to ear. *Uh oh.*

"Who is *Camila*? Why has Noah met her and not me?"

I shift uncomfortably in my chair. Even Dad is eyeing me from over his newspaper at the table in the breakfast nook.

"Just my paralegal."

I round the counter and snag a piece of bacon from behind Mom's back before she can stop me. She frowns.

"Your paralegal? And you went out drinking with her to the point of having a hangover?"

Dad folds his paper and clears his throat.

"Your mother's right, son. Mixing business and pleasure is never a good idea."

I catch myself before I roll my eyes; Dad doesn't tolerate disrespect.

"C'mon, Dad. There was no *pleasure*. We just ran into each other at The Commodore and Noah invited her and her sister to join us for drinks."

Dad doesn't look convinced. He shares a look with Mom, who's all but forgotten the pancakes.

"Well...make sure it stays that way. Not only can things get tricky when you get close to people you work with, but you should know there's a legal risk as well."

This time I do roll my eyes. Talk about blowing things out of proportion. Dad's frown deepens.

"Nothing happened. You think my paralegal's going to sue me because we had a few drinks? That happens at most client lunches and you know that."

Rather than stick around to head the end of Dad's lecture, I pull my phone out and text Murray. Time to head back to Westchester. It's a shame I'll have to miss those pancakes. Nothing's better to soak up last night's bad decisions.

I come behind Dad's chair to give him a pat on the back before walking over to kiss Mom on the cheek.

"Listen, Murrary's on his way and I still need to shower." I head towards the stairs and Mom suddenly looks worried.

"You're still coming tomorrow for family dinner, right?"

I turn and give her my most reassuring smile.

"Of course, Mom. I wouldn't miss it."

After a shower and a fresh change of clothes, I feel human again. I made Murray stop at Burger King for my greasy hangover remedy, and that plus two Excedrin finally conquered that beast of a headache. *Thank God!* I couldn't fucking think.

Before I can settle into the back of the Navigator for the long drive down I-95, my phone dings.

Noah

Noah: Hey, bro. Thanks for coming out last night!

No problem, man. Honestly, I probably needed it more than you.

Noah: Is this Henry? Henry Park, Jr.? Partner at BYOB? Since when does the worst workaholic I know ever need to go out for drinks?

You're such a dick. You know it's BBS&P.

Noah: Oh, I definitely know. I just like annoying you.

Alright. See you at Mom and Dad's to-morrow

Noah: Wait wait wait! I'm just kidding. Damn, bro.

Noah: What happened? Why did you need a drink?

I debate whether I should even tell him. *What good will it even do to talk about it?* But Noah is one of the few people who knows the full history of the situation.

Noah

We got a new client yesterday, too.

Noah: And? Don't leave me hanging, bro!

It's Naomi.

Noah: ???

Naomi Watanabe. The girl I was thinking of getting serious with in law school.

And she looked *good*. *Really good*. Why couldn't she have had the common decency to show up with a terrible haircut or missing a few teeth?

Noah: Oh shit, bro. That's rough.

I sigh. "Oh shit" is right.

Noah

Even worse? Her soon to be ex is that fuckin cum stain, Tanner

Noah: Tanner?! That dude was a hookup at best and she MARRIED him?

I smile to myself. He may be a pain in the ass, but Noah has always had my back.

Noah

LOL. Tell me about it.

So, if I seem a little on edge for the next few months, now you know why.

Noah: You got this, bro.

Noah: Anyway, I'm sure Camila could help take the edge off.

I look at my phone like it's grown legs. What's Camila got to do with anything?

Noah

Uh…Yeah. She's a great paralegal.

Noah: LOL! A great paralegal? What are you talking about, bro?

What are YOU talking about?

Noah: Wow. You're really going to play dumb?

Please. Enlighten me as to what I'm missing.

Noah: That woman wants your dick, bro. BAD.

Noah: And from the look on your face when Rory and I left, the feeling was mutual.

So much for always having my back. Now he sounds like Mom and Dad!

Noah

Everything between me and Camila is professional.

I toss my phone on the neighboring seat and let my head fall back against the seat. Why is everyone so sure I crossed the line with Camila? Sure, she's beautiful. Even hidden under those cheap cardigans and too-long skirts, I'm guessing she's got a killer body. I've even seen glimpses of it over the years. But she works for me and never once have I let our attraction go anywhere. There's no way I would let my control slip now, not after all these years.

Once I get home, I attempt to skip my routine like I had at Mom and Dad's, but no dice. And after an hour on the treadmill, a hot shower, tea, and some unusually rigorous masturbation, I finally pass out asleep.

From the warmth of my cocoon, awash in blackness, I see her. Features slowly come into focus. Full red lips. Eyes as dark as the strongest espresso. Soft, round hips hidden beneath a sensible black skirt. Firm breasts that arch into my palm as she whimpers into my mouth. My hands pull her closer against me, close enough to feel her heart racing under my touch. I'm sweeping loose tendrils aside, gripping her throat, angling her mouth until it's at my mercy.

I wake up with a start before my alarm can even go off. The pounding in my head is nothing compared to the ache in the pit of my stomach. Everyone was right. I *did* cross the line.

CHAPTER TEN

Camila

"It's not safe for you to take the subway at this hour, Camila," Henry says. His concern strokes something deep under my skin, raising goosebumps on my arm.

"It's fine," I protest. "I'm a big girl. Plus, I carry a stun gun in my purse."

At that, he chuckles lightly, raising his hand to tuck a wayward curl behind my ear.

"Of course. I know you're a grown woman, Camila. Plump and juicy and just begging for someone to take a bite."

"Mr. Park!" I gasp, taken aback at his boldness.

His hand, still behind my ear, clutches the back of my neck firmly and brings my mouth so close we share the same breath.

"That's right, Camila. Call me 'Mr. Park'. 'Mr. Park', your demanding, unreasonable boss. Never forget that I'm in charge. I can make you work until midnight tonight. I can bend you to my will. And right now, my will is to bend you over this desk, and spread those caramel thighs."

Fitting words to actions, he swiftly turns me to face his desk, forces my head down onto this morning's client files, and kicks my feet apart. *Shit!* I couldn't be wetter if I dove into the deep end of a pool. I'm definitely in the deep end now.

I keep my eyes focused on the Waterman pen near his keyboard as his hand skims up my inner thigh, higher and higher until he reaches the lace of my stockings. The friction of the lace against the pads of his fingers starts an itch inside me that I will *beg* him to scratch if I have to. *This can't be just a tease.* He lets out a groan that sounds like it's through clenched teeth.

"Tsk tsk, Camila. This whole time, you've been hiding seductive thigh highs under here? You know I've got to punish you for that."

I bite my bottom lip to keep from moaning and grip the edge of the desk tighter. He laughs at my silence.

"That's fine. You won't be able to stay quiet for long, Mila. Not when I push up this ridiculous skirt and slap these luscious cheeks of yours. Not when I fall to my knees and bury my face in that streaming cunt I can already feel radiating through your panties. Not when I slide a finger deep in your pussy to match the rhythm of my tongue on your clit, biting down until you're nearly crazy with need. You won't be able to stay quiet then. But sure, do your best."

Ever the cocky asshole. I can actually *hear* him smirking. I can't wait to make him eat his words...and other things. I keep my lips firmly trapped between my teeth, my breath coming out of my nostrils in desperate gusts.

"Camila."

I stay silent, patiently waiting for him to touch me, to brand me with his fingers, his tongue. To drive into me so deep he can feel my soul.

"Camila?"

He's taunting me now, trying to get me to surrender. I won't speak. I won't turn around. If he wants me, he must take me.

"Camila, are you OK?"

A tentative hand lands on my shoulder, and I nearly fall out of my chair. I'm not on Henry's desk. I'm not even in Henry's office. Instead of Henry, Jeremy from the mailroom is hovering over my desk while I have the most vivid daydream of my life. Jeremy can't be more than twenty—with a mop of unruly red hair, a beard that refuses to grow in evenly, and stubborn acne—and I'm traumatizing the poor kid. I clear my throat and focus my eyes on his, hoping he doesn't notice the embarrassed blush on my cheeks.

"Jeremy, hi! Sorry, I was kinda spacing out there."

He looks at me doubtfully, but drops the certified mail on my desk.

"You asked for the envelope from Tanner Moore as soon as it arrived."

I take it with a smile.

"Thanks so much. I owe you a beer for bringing it to me directly."

He rolls his eyes, but returns my smile.

"Don't worry about it. When would you even have the time? I know Sub Zero never lets you have any fun."

"What's that, Jeremy?"

At the sound of Henry's voice behind him, Jeremy's back goes rigid and his smile falters. He doesn't dare turn around.

"Nothing, sir. My apologies, sir."

Still refusing to make eye contact, Jeremy backs away before breaking into a sprint when he reaches the end of the hall. I turn to Henry with a raised eyebrow.

"Was that really necessary?"

Henry's face is unreadable.

"Please have a seat in my office, Ms. Sanchez."

Huh. So we're back to Ms. Sanchez. Pen and pad in hand, I follow him inside and shut the door behind me.

"Henry, you probably scared Jeremy to death. He was—"

"In the office, you will address me as Mr. Park."

The iciness in his tone lets me know this isn't playful banter, and I bite back my sarcastic reply.

"Of course, Mr. Park."

"I asked you in here," he begins, walking around his desk and taking a seat, "to clear the air about last week."

Oh, this oughta be good. I take a seat in one of the armchairs in the sitting area.

"Clear the air?"

"Yes. What happened last week was wildly inappropriate and it won't be happening again."

My shoulders sag the tiniest bit.

"I see."

"As you know, I have rules about interoffice relationships. Rules that have served me well for many years."

So he gets to put his tongue down my throat, squeeze my tits, and then on Monday there are rules? *Well, I've certainly heard enough.* I click my pen closed and stand.

"I understand, Mr. Park. There's no need to discuss it further. Will that be all?"

For a split second, he looks surprised before quickly smoothing his features. He clearly expected an argument. I don't dare give him the satisfaction. I'll beg him to reconsider the same day I'm crowned the next Queen of England.

"Yes. That will be all. Thank you, Ms. Sanchez."

I'm out of his office before my name has finished passing his lips, slamming the door a bit too hard and stomping to my desk.

The nerve of that guy! He thinks he can kiss me and touch me and then just say forget it? Fuck him, and fuck BBS&P!

Back at my desk, I pull up my calendar. *No more meetings today.* Perfect.

I rage-file the pile of client documents sitting on my desk, snatch up my purse, and fly down the hallway to the elevator. I ignore the strange looks the other paralegals give me and jam the down button. A wise bystander senses my dark mood and opts to take the next elevator down.

The doors close and I hurriedly type out a text.

I'm sorry, Mr. Park. But I think I am coming down with something. There are no more meetings today, so I'm taking the afternoon off to rest. I hope to be back tomorrow.

I don't wait for a response and dial the top number in my favorites. She answers after one ring and I talk over her greeting.

"Rory? Where are you? I got the afternoon off and I'm coming to surprise you on set."

"I love you, Jess. I think I've always loved you, even when we fought. Even when I pushed you away. We were meant to be."

The dashing brunette actor pours his heart out to a leggy blonde while a rain machine mists the entire set. I roll my eyes. *What a load of bullshit.*

"I knew if I waited long enough, you would realize. Knew you would finally see me."

Finally see you? Why wouldn't a guy see a woman who looks like she could be on the cover of Vanity Fair? This is so unrealistic.

"I *do* see you. I saw you from the beginning; I was just too scared to act on it. I didn't think I was good enough for you."

An unladylike snort escapes my lips, and Rory cuts her eyes at me in warning. *Shit.*

"You're here now. *We're* here now. That's all that matters."

The two actors embrace in a passionate kiss. In post-production, I'm sure there will be a big swell of violins and piano, marking the beginning of their epic love story.

"And cut! Let's take fifteen, people!" the director yells. He looks, at most, twenty-five. *What does he know about love?*

Before I can further pick apart this train wreck of a movie, Rory yanks me out of my chair and far enough down the street that we're out of earshot of anyone in the production.

"Big sis, I love you, but what the fuck is going on? You've been sucking your teeth and rolling your eyes ever since you got here."

She looks pissed, and rightfully so. I may not care if Henry fires me,—he probably already has; I haven't checked my phone since I left—but that's no reason to mess with my kid sister's money.

"Sorry, Rory. I'll chill."

She looks at me with concern and pulls me to sit next to her on the railing of a nearby apartment building.

"That's not what I asked. What's going on with you? Did something happen?"

I sigh, resigned that I have to reveal my embarrassment. That I have to *relive* it while it's still tender and red.

"Friday, after everyone left, when it was just Henry and I?" She nods, urging me to continue. "Well, we kinda...made out."

"Made out! Holy shit! I had a feeling you had the hots for him, even though you tried to act like you hated him."

"I never tried to act like I hated him," I interrupt, hating the defensiveness in my voice. "He *is* a strict boss. He's got all these rules, and he makes me work late almost every night, and—"

"And you *like* him. Don't deny it. Was the kiss hot? Was it a Hallmark kiss or an HBO Max kiss?"

I giggle at my sister. She's always gotta have the juicy details.

"Definitely an HBO Max kiss. Maybe even Pay Per View. God, the man really knows his way around a mouth."

Rory smiles wickedly.

"And? Did you ask him to come back to your place to do the horizontal tango? Does he know his way around a pussy, too?"

I playfully elbow her in the ribs and she grips the railing to keep from falling.

"No! Nothing like that. We just kissed. He had his driver take me home and crashed with his family in Brooklyn. But today, after a whole weekend of thinking about it and hoping it will go somewhere, he calls me into his office and says it was a mistake. Says it can't happen again. It breaks one of his precious rules."

I keep the tear in my eye with sheer force of will and Rory leans her head on my shoulder.

"Oh, sis. I'm sorry. That sucks."

"Yeah. I didn't actually get the afternoon off; I just left. I couldn't stay there feeling like a fool."

"I get it. I would've left too, right after I kneed him in the balls"

I sniffle and give her a small smile.

"I know. I was channelling you."

She raises an eyebrow.

"You kneed him in the balls?"

I can't help but laugh.

"No. The *leaving* part, not the *misdemeanor assault* part. I work at a law firm, remember?"

I take a deep breath, glad the threat of tears is gone.

"Anyway, I actually might not work at that law firm after pulling that little stunt. I was just...so...mad. I thought he was finally loosening up, but no! Same old Sub Zero."

Rory pats me on the back and holds out her hand.

"First, let's check whether you still have a job. You said you texted him?"

I place my phone in her palm.

"Yeah. I told him I was coming down with something."

She grins as she enters my passcode.

"Classic. I'm looking...I don't see anything from Henry in here." She locks my phone and hands it back to me. "Let's assume no news is good news."

"OK. But what about tomorrow? And the day after that? Shit, it's only Monday!"

"First off, breathe. You've got a great job, you're smart, and you're super sexy. Tomorrow, and every day following, you are going to torture him."

"Torture him?"

"Yes. You are going to wear the sexiest outfits you have. The tightest skirts, the highest heels, the lowest-cut tops. As scandalous as BBS&P's dress code allows. You're going to stop with this *old maid, no makeup* bullshit and put on some lipstick and mascara. You are going to make him salivate every time he sees you, but you are going to completely ignore him."

While outlining her master plan, Rory jumps up, pacing and gesticulating. She truly is an evil genius. Thank goodness she's on *my* side.

"Do I want to know how you came up with this plan so quickly?"

"No. No, you do not."

I laugh to myself and stand up, pulling her in for a big hug.

"I thought *I* was supposed to be the big sister."

She hugs me back, and I can hear the sincerity in her voice.

"You *are* the big sister. And there's no way Gabe and I can repay you for taking care of us after...after everything. I'm just glad I can lend you my revenge skills to get even. It sounds like Henry really deserves it."

I step back and give her a mischievous grin.

"Oh, you have *no* idea." We link arms and start walking back to the set. "I hope I can raid your closet. After years at BBS&P, I've got nothing that could make anyone salivate."

She jumps excitedly and claps her hands together.

"Yay! Makeover!"

CHAPTER ELEVEN

Henry

I read her text for the tenth time and try to ignore the sheen of sweat dampening the back of my dress shirt. That could not have gone worse. *Please, God, don't let me lose the best paralegal in the firm over a harmless kiss!*

I lean back in my chair, close my eyes, and remember the way it felt to pull her against me. The pleasant give of her hips in my hands. How my mouth watered when I felt her nipples tighten through her shirt. The sexy whimpers that raised the hairs on my arms. *Harmless, my ass*. That kiss was hotter than some sex I've had. And now that I've felt her, I can't *un-feel* her. I'll always be thinking about it, especially if she's going to keep stomping around here, making her perfect ass shake sensually. *Deep breaths, Henry.*

I would've followed her. Maybe I should have. Despite her impressive poker face, I knew she was upset, but the lead pipe in my pants meant I had to stay seated. Bits and pieces of my dream—of what happened between us—kept flashing in my head, even while she was glaring at me, and I doubt chasing after her with a divining rod pointed right at her would've helped my "let's keep things professional" argument. Letting her run out of here and pretending I bought the sick excuse was definitely for the best. *But she wouldn't stay out tomorrow too, would she?*

I pretend I can't see the mounting emails in my inbox and press the first button on my speed dial.

"Henry Park, Jr., attorney at law, calling his baby brother during *work* hours? Did someone die?"

My God, Noah is a smug bastard.

"You're younger by six minutes, dick. Cut the 'baby brother' bullshit." He'd said something similar at the bar, and it rubbed me the wrong way then, too.

"One sec."

On the other side of the phone, I can hear him rustling papers on his desk. Once he's back on the line, his tone is much more sincere.

"So, based on your agitated tone and the unheard-of midday call, I'm guessing something really *is* wrong. Is it Mom or Dad? Is it Mom *and* Dad? Jesus, tell me the rest of brothers are OK."

"Noah!" I interrupt. He's spiraling. "Calm down and stop guessing. Mom and Dad are fine. It's nothing family-related."

I hear the distinct squeak of an office chair as he leans back. Smug Noah has returned.

"So if it's not family, and since you've never called me about work before, this means it's personal. Is it romantic?"

I don't answer right away. Kissing Camila was nice. Scratch that; it was *hot*. But it was lust, not *romance*. I rake my fingers through my hair.

"Not romantic, no. I just...When you left, Camila and I..." I can barely say it. What kind of scum crosses the line with his subordinate? *The kind that wants to fuck her*, Evil Jiminy Cricket whispers in the back of my head. On the other end of the line, Noah gasps.

"Y'all hooked up?! Congrats, bro! I knew she was feeling you. I gave her my best lines and got nothing."

I feel the tension in my shoulders ratchet higher.

"You were never going to *get* anything. Save your tired lines for someone else," I growl. Noah laughs in response.

"Hooking up with hot paralegals *and* getting jealous? Am I speaking to Henry? Blink twice if you've been body snatched."

I roll my eyes.

"First off, you couldn't see me even if I did blink. Second, Camila and I didn't hook up. We just...made out a little. I may have felt her up...slightly. I sent her home alone and spent the night at Mom and Dad's."

Noah goes from teasing to bored in 0.5 seconds flat.

"Please tell me you didn't interrupt prep for my meeting with Yeon Woo-jin to talk about a kiss. What's next? Are you gonna pass her a note during study hall? Leave a rose in her locker? Just take the woman out to dinner like a man."

I let out an exasperated breath. It's going to take *two* hours on the treadmill to wind down tonight.

"You know I can't do that, Noah. She *works* for me. I told her it couldn't happen again, and then she stormed off. She sent me a text saying she's sick, but I know that's bullshit. What am I going to do?"

I can practically picture him shrugging in response to my borderline whine. Noah Park, the very picture of empathy.

"You've got me, bro. Let's conference in Adam and Cory. Maybe they've got experience with this sort of thing."

Before I can stop him, he clicks over to add the calls. After two minutes, Noah's back on the line with Cory.

"So you got your secretary pregnant, man? That's a bold move."

I nearly choke on my tongue.

"What?!" I sputter. "Is that what Noah told you?"

"Close enough," Cory drawls.

Another minute later and Noah is back with Adam.

"This better be good, guys. Maya and I were just about to—"

Adam breaks off abruptly, and Cory and Noah both laugh knowingly. Even I crack a smile. Ever since Adam popped the question to Maya, they've been joined at the hip. Disappearing upstairs at every family dinner. Coming back downstairs with inside-out clothes and missing buttons. It's so sweet I could vomit.

"Anyway," Adam says awkwardly.

"So why did you call this Council of the Bros, Noah? I gotta be back at work in ten minutes." Cory's always been one to cut straight to the point.

"Junior here made out with his hot paralegal and now he's worried she's going to call HR on him," Noah responds.

Cory's laugh fills the line.

"*Perfect* Henry, Jr. broke a cardinal rule of the bachelor pact? You pushed 'don't shit where you eat' more than any of us, man. How ironic."

"Seems to me like he was trying to keep exactly this from happening," Adam teases. I am not amused.

"Look, guys. You can make fun of me later. Right now, I need to know what to do. She basically ran out of here with just a text on her way out the door. I don't even know if she's coming back in tomorrow."

Adam whistles.

"Damn. She sounds pretty mad. You sure all you did was make out?"

I hear Adam's phone jostle before Maya's warm voice comes on the line.

"Hey, boys."

"Hello, Maya," we all chorus in response.

"What's this I hear about 'making out'?"

"Apparently Henry, Jr. made out with his assistant," Adam offers from beside Maya. She must have switched to speaker phone.

"Wow. 'Mr. Straight and Narrow' is breaking the rules, huh? Be careful. First you kiss your assistant and next you'll be turning to a life of crime." I can hear the humor in her voice.

Et tu, Brute? Just for that, she and Adam are only getting a set of dish towels from their registry.

"Camila's not my assistant; she's my paralegal," I explain. If I'm welcoming my entire family into my personal life, they should at least have the facts straight. "We had a few too many drinks celebrating with Noah and kissed a little. No big deal."

From Maya's squeal, I can tell she's making it a big deal.

"Ooh! Making out with the boss. That is so hot."

"Maya, babe. Please don't use the word 'hot' in any context that includes my brother."

"Oh stop, Adam. I'm just saying, interoffice romances can be pretty..." She chooses her next words carefully. "Appealing. At least for some."

"'Appealing' is definitely not the word I would use for something that opens me up to a sexual harassment lawsuit."

"Oh, boo!" Cory shouts into the phone.

"Do you really think she would do that, Henry?" Maya asks. Thank God *someone* on this call has a little compassion.

"Honestly, I don't know. But it was a stupid mistake. Even if she doesn't call HR, it's probably going to impact our work dynamic."

"Boo!" Cory shouts again, louder this time.

"You've worked with this woman for what? Five years?" *Six, but who's counting?* "I doubt she's going to narc on you after a little kiss. She probably already thought about it before it happened." Cory might be a bit of a dick, but he's making sense. Has Camila wanted to get together this whole time?

"Man, this is getting good, but do you think you guys can wrap this call up in the next ten minutes? I'm under a tight deadline for some bridesmaid totes, and I really need Adam's help with the silk screen."

"Yes, ma'am," we chorus again. Adam takes his phone off speaker.

"You heard her. I can't keep the lady waiting," Adam says. "So what do you need, Henry?"

I furrow my brow in thought. *What* do *I need?* They can't erase what happened last Friday. I wouldn't want them to. But they are right. You don't shit where you eat. I sigh.

"I don't really know that anything can be done. Just keep your fingers crossed that I'm not in HR by the end of the week."

"Or," Cory chimes in. "You can play extra nice at work, and maybe she'll drop the whole thing."

"Extra nice?" I question skeptically. "I'm her boss. I'm not there to be nice."

Adam chuckles.

"Those sound like the words of someone about to get written up. I agree with Cory. Don't harass her or anything. Just be nicer."

"We all know you can be a bit stiff, bro," adds Noah. "Loosen up, play nice, and hopefully, this all blows over."

I hope to God they're right. I don't have time to hire and train someone new right now. I'm right in the middle of Naomi's case and I can't screw up with a VIP. *Loosen up. Play nice.* That's going to be my motto until things cool down.

"Maybe I'll stop keeping her so late? Bring in some donuts or something?"

Noah laughs.

"Hearing you figure out how to be nice is like watching monkeys try to use tools."

I hang up at the sound of my brothers' laughter. I can tell I'm never going to live this conversation down.

Chapter Twelve

Henry

I'm at a loss. After a night of fretting, it's like yesterday never happened. Camila didn't show up late. She didn't stomp when I called her into my office to discuss outstanding invoices. She didn't roll her eyes or glare when we reviewed the last of the client files moving to archive, even though I had several questions and she's been trying to close out this task for weeks. She's been professional to a T.

Unfortunately, she also didn't drink the iced caramel frappuccino with extra whip I left on her desk before she got in this morning. Byron at Starbucks thought I had a screw loose when I ordered it with my usual black coffee. My first attempt to "play nice" is now up for grabs in the communal kitchen. At least *someone* will enjoy it.

I should be jumping for joy. After all, I probably don't have to worry about getting a slap on the wrist from HR. I probably do, however, need to switch my nightly hot showers to cold.

Gone are the frumpy K-Mart suits my aunt could've worn. Instead, Camila's wearing a form fitting pencil skirt and four-inch stilettos. She traded her worn out cardigan for a blouse that plunges so low I can see the magenta lace of her bra whenever she leans over my desk. Her usual no-nonsense buns and ponytails have been replaced with loose, wavy locks long enough to brush the tops of her breasts. If we didn't work together, I'd be thinking about running my fingers through her tresses, feeling the silkiness against my skin and envisioning it wrapped around my fist. Since we work together, though, that's the furthest thing from my mind.

On the second day after "the storm out", she wears a cream wrap dress that stops above the knees to reveal shapely legs and another pair of stilettos. Her hair is down again, but pulled back from her face to highlight gold hoop earrings that brush against the long column of her neck any time she talks. It's borderline distracting. The skin there looks smooth and sensitive. Is something I would say if we weren't colleagues.

Walking into Naomi and Tanner's first mediation, I almost bump into Camila when she bends down to pick up papers from her leather folio. *No more plain legal pad for her.* It takes almost all of my concentration not to think about what someone who *doesn't* work with her would think after seeing the outline of a thong against her tight navy skirt. Someone who *doesn't* work with her might think about sliding that skirt up to expose the plump, lush globes, pushing that thong to the side, and—

"Shall we begin, counselor?"

Both the mediator and stenographer look at me expectantly, and I clear my throat to regain some self-control. Camila raises an eyebrow in question.

"Yes, of course. Please proceed."

I open my copy of the client file to validate Tanner's answers and ensure Naomi does not needlessly disclose anything that could impact the settlement. As we anticipated, the largest liability is the pending TanFit IPO. Most judges would question a spouse filing for divorce so close to when the other stands to receive a windfall. I'll need to prep Naomi for hostile questioning from the other attorney on this.

Despite the awkward start, the mediation proceeds as expected. Tanner flew out to attend in person, and both he and Naomi appear calm throughout. But I don't miss the tic in Tanner's jaw each time property is discussed. Years as a divorce attorney means I have a nose for when a client is trying to withhold information. I make a note to investigate further.

It's been two weeks since the incident and Camila hasn't slipped and called me "Henry" once. She comes in on time and works diligently, but doesn't stay a second past when I dismiss her to go home. She's even pushed back against staying late once or twice, mentioning "after-work commitments". *Does she have a hot date or something?*

She used to ask about my weekend, offer to grab me a coffee, tease me about my repetitive lunch orders. All of that's gone and in its place is painfully dry small talk. The weather. Her commute. The date of the next department happy hour. And now *I'm* the one initiating these conversations, if you can call them that. They last no longer than is polite before she's back at her desk or off to the library for more research.

With everyone else, she's her usual chatty self. She led this month's paralegal professional development session, lingering in the conference room to joke around with the team before heading out for drinks. When she's at her desk, she's talking and laughing with anyone that passes by; usually that dweeb, Jeremy, from the mailroom. They laugh together *a lot*. He finds a reason to visit her desk almost daily, bringing her packages as soon as they arrive or volunteering to help her stuff envelopes. She's too blind to see the poor boy's got a crush on her. I wish it didn't all unfold in full view of my desk.

All the coffees, bagels, and muffins I've left for her have ended up in the kitchen for some hungry interns to pilfer.

A month has passed since our little incident and I'm starting to feel twitchy. Today, she's wearing a forest green dress with buttons down the front and a matching belt. Her arms are bare and her supple, honey-tinged skin seems to glow even in the fluorescent lights of the office. Long, full lashes surround round eyes so dark and deep I could fall into them. I can't believe just four weeks ago I thought this woman looked plain. She's *beautiful*. Distractingly so.

Still, I want the old Camila back. The one who asked personal questions I always dodged. The one who noticed when something was off that first day with Naomi. The one who brought me that gift basket for Christmas during COVID. The one who called me Henry even when I corrected her. The one who hid her dangerous curves under knee-length skirts, sensible pumps, and loose sweaters.

This Camila doesn't do any of that. This new, aloof, sexy Camila is currently on her hands and knees behind my desk doing God knows what. Plugging in a new router, perhaps? Certainly not what my sex-starved brain is *imagining* she's doing. I clear my throat to stop her before those thoughts tighten the crotch of my pants any further.

"Ms. Sanchez. May I ask what you're doing?"

Down on all fours, she looks back at me over her shoulder and my throat constricts.

"I dropped my pen and the dang thing rolled all the way under your desk. I'll be out of your hair in a minute, Mr. Park."

Please take your time. I'll just wait here thinking about baseball statistics and trying not to drool. After a final arch of her back,—the memory of which I will definitely revisit before bed tonight—she starts to stand, but her killer heels buckle on the way up; Louboutin is hardly made for crawling.

Unable to find her footing, she stumbles into me, pressing her entire front against *my* entire front. And she feels it. She feels...*me.* Evidence I *really* enjoyed her little floor show is currently straining against the inside of my zipper and attempting to stab her in the belly button. *Oh God.* Her eyes widen in recognition just as I push away from the contact.

"Pardon me, sir. I-I'll just head back to my desk."

She scurries out of my office and shuts the door behind her. *Well, shit.* As if things weren't awkward enough, now I'm getting hard-ons in the office like a teenager. I yank my phone out of my pocket to text Noah.

Noah

Camila just felt my boner!

Noah: Yo, what? LOL

I came into my office and Camila was on her knees under my desk

Noah: Hot. I've seen videos that start like that.

Oh grow up

I was nowhere near her when she was down there, but then she tripped and fell right into me.

Noah: LOL!!!

Noah: OK. So why are you talking to me?

Noah: You should be playing naughty secretary with her right now!

I wish, but she ran out of here so fast, she left skid marks on the carpet

Noah: Oof.

It was bad, man. Things have been off since we made out. Now she's probably going to ask for a transfer

Noah: I'm sorry, bro.

Noah: You think maybe she didn't like what she felt?

What?

Noah: Like maybe Dad only passed the sundae down to me ;-)

You know for a fact that's not true

Noah: I won't tell the other brothers if that's what you're worried about

Noah: I've read men with micropenises can still go on to lead healthy, fulfilling lives.

OMG. Whoever said twins have some special bond was full of shit.

Well, *that* was a waste. Now Mila thinks I'm some pervert and my brother's going to rub this in my face for the next three months at least. I bet he's already sent screenshots of our texts to Cory.

I clench my jaw and pound my fist on the desk. *Fuck this!* Acting like I don't find her attractive isn't working. "Playing nice" *definitely* isn't working. It's time I faced this head on. We're both adults, and if she wants to transfer to another department, so be it.

Resolved to accept whatever happens, I press the intercom button.

"Ms. Sanchez? Can you please come into my office?"

I wait five seconds and there's no answer.

"Ms. Sanchez? May I have a word?"

A few more seconds go by and still nothing. I push out of my seat, cross my office, and open my door, only to see her desk empty. *Don't tell me she's run off again!* I pull my phone out, checking for another bogus text. Nothing. I let out a breath, thankful for the small victory. I have to find her. I'm beyond ready to put this whole mess behind us.

I walk past conference rooms and the other partners' offices, checking up and down hallways until I'm standing outside the file room. It's dim and cramped,—we need to have an intern clean this out immediately—but I see her, standing on her tiptoes to reach a box on the top shelf. The image she makes is so alluring, I move without consciously deciding to do so.

"Here. Let me get that for you," I say. Reaching over her head, I'm close enough to touch her. Close enough to smell her perfume; it's something vanilla with a musky edge. Maybe sandalwood?

When I place the box on the table beside her, I don't immediately move away. I should. Camila and I in a dimly lit room—a room with a lock on the door—is not a good idea. She looks up at me and I see her eyes dilate.

"Thank you," she whispers.

I take a deep breath. Now's the moment of truth.

"Mila, I think we need to discuss what's been going on."

She gasps, staring at me with wide eyes.

"What?"

"It's just that you always call me 'Ms. Sanchez' at the office. I believe it's one of your *rules.*"

She spits the last word out like it leaves a sour taste in her mouth. *Shit. Did I really just call her 'Mila'?*

"My apologies, Ms. Sanchez. The fact remains that we need to discuss the change in our work dynamic."

She rolls her eyes and reaches for the box.

"If you're about to give me the whole 'let's keep things professional' speech, I'll remind you that you're the one who crossed the line in your office just now."

I rake my hands through my hair in frustration.

"That was an accident. You're the one who was on all fours looking like a damn pinup."

I close and lock the door so anyone still around doesn't overhear our conversation. Mila starts angrily yanking files from the box.

"A pinup, huh? So, are you saying I was asking for it?"

Yikes. Did that really come out of my mouth?

"I just mean your clothes lately are hardly work appropriate."

She turns to skewer me with a glare hot enough to melt steel.

"I'll have you know, Mr. Park, that all of my outfits adhere to BBS&P's strict wardrobe policy. I checked."

Mila huffs and turns back to the files.

"Ms. Sanchez, we're still talking."

She whirls around to face me, rage coming off her in waves.

"You're not *talking*. You're *yelling* at me. Laying down the law like you always do with no consideration for the other person in the conversation. This isn't the courtroom, Mr. Park."

This conversation is going worse than the last time. It's time to switch tactics.

"You're right," I admit. "This isn't the courtroom, and you should have a say."

She looks so surprised by my agreement, I wonder if I've really been "playing nice" at all.

"Well..." she starts hesitantly, "quit buying me coffees and snacks and stuff. You never did that before and it's weirding me out."

Ouch.

"OK..."

"And if I end the conversation to get back to work, stop pushing me to keep talking. I'm allowed to feel a little weird about what happened before things get back to normal."

"OK. I was just trying to—"

"I know what you were trying to do, but be real. You can't make out with me on Friday, call things off on Monday, and expect everything to be back to normal on Tuesday."

"Ms. Sanchez, I didn't call things off. Things were never *on*."

She steps towards me, poking an angry finger into my chest.

"Oh no? So making out with me, feeling me up, and then letting me take your car home meant nothing to you?"

"I didn't say—"

"Or are you blaming it on the alcohol?"

"I *did* have quite a lot of—"

She lets out an unladylike snort and resumes her angry filing.

"Got it. The only way you can make out with the chubby paralegal is when you're blackout drunk."

The blood in my veins goes ice cold. I step into her personal space; close enough for her to feel my breath against her lips.

"I said I would hear you out. I did *not* say I would let you talk shit about me or yourself."

Camila remains silent, sensing the danger in my voice.

"I had a lot of drinks that night, sure, but I think what just happened in my office proves I'm attracted to you with or without the alcohol."

The tempo of her breath picks up, pushing her breasts into my chest. At the feel of her against me, all sense flies from my head.

"The alcohol may have made me forget the rules, but it had nothing to do with why I kissed you that night."

Her pupils are big as saucers, and laser focused on my mouth.

"Oh? So why did you kiss me?"

"I—"

She steps closer to me, her breasts pressed so tightly against my chest now that I can feel her pebble hard nipples through her blouse. *Why did I come in here, again?*

"What made you put your hands on my hips that night? Why did you grab my neck and push your tongue into my mouth?"

Her last words are whispered against my neck, her lips grazing my skin. I close my eyes to try and block out her assault of my senses.

"Camila..."

"Yes, Henry?"

She presses her lips firmly to the side of my jaw, dragging them up to the shell of my ear before she first bites, then licks the tender flesh. *Fuck the rules.*

I let out a growl before taking her neck just as I did that night, finding her mouth open and yielding to my lips and tongue. I'm drowning in her erotic scents: her perfume, the tangy smell of her arousal, the mint of her breath as she pants into my mouth.

I release the hand on the back of her neck to explore the delectable tits driving me senseless. My knuckles brush her skin as I unbutton one button on her dress, then a second, then a third, until only thin, black lace covers her chest.

Unable to resist looking at the treasure I've revealed, I break the kiss and stare unabashedly right at her breasts. Her coffee-colored nipples push against her bra, begging me to touch them, to lick them, to worship them.

Who am I to deny her?

I kiss along the rim of the lace, descending further into madness with each whimper that leaves Camila's mouth. She's just as responsive as I remember.

Finally, I thumb the lace aside and pinch a point between my lips, swirling it against my tongue like the most sinful truffle. She clutches my shoulders with each lick, using my chest to muffle her moans.

My erection is pushing against her, so ready to sink into her, I feel the first drops of precum leave the tip. I nudge my knee between her legs and can't stifle a groan at the feel of her steaming core through the fabric of my pants.

The sound of someone trying the door before realizing it's locked—*thank God!*—turns us both to stone. How do we explain this? Camila recovers first, stepping away and yanking her nipple from my mouth with a moist pop. Her abrupt retreat thankfully works like ice water, deflating my cock in the same time it takes her to pick up the box of files, paste a smile on her face, and thrust open the door.

"Oops! The door must've closed behind me!" she says too brightly to whoever waits on the other side.

As she pushes the door open wider to make her escape, I see it's a member of the cleaning crew. My heart resumes beating and I make a note to drop a couple Benjamins in the collection plate this Sunday. Things with Camila just went from awkward to *beyond* complicated.

CHAPTER THIRTEEN

Camila

Yesterday was way too close for comfort. If it had been anyone but Jorge in maintenance, we would both be in deep shit. I can't deny I like Henry—how can I not?—but no one's going to hire a brand new lawyer that was fired from BBS&P for inappropriate conduct.

I wait in the plush leather chairs in his office and check my watch for the fiftieth time this morning. I got in at seven after spending most of last night pretending to sleep. How was I supposed to sleep when every time I closed my eyes, I saw his burning into me? I tasted the need in every swipe of his tongue, heard the desire in the moans he tried to contain. If not for the interruption, I might have let him take me right on the file table.

Might have? the slutty voice in my head counters. *If not for Jorge, you'd be at CVS picking up Plan B right now.* Thankfully, cooler heads prevailed, followed by an even colder shower when I got home.

At least the attraction is mutual, even if we can't act on it. I'll probably need earplugs to protect against the deafening *I told you so*'s from Rory once I tell her how well her clothes worked, but it'll be worth it considering Henry and I's little closet rendezvous is going to keep me warm for many nights to come. I'll just buy some AAAs along with the earplugs.

I look up at the sound of Henry's door opening. He sees me sitting and a smile so warm it heats my insides spreads across his face. God, he's not going to make this easy.

"Good morning, Camila."

I bite my lips to contain a gasp. I'm still not used to being anything but "Ms. Sanchez" to him. *His* Ms. Sanchez.

"Good morning, sir. Why don't you have a seat so we can talk?"

His smile turns chagrined as he takes the seat across from mine.

"Uh oh. Is it *my* turn to get the brush off now? I bet I can change your mind if you give me a chance."

He winks and my heart stutters. I cannot handle Flirty Henry. *¡Dios mío, give me strength!*

I laugh awkwardly and struggle to maintain eye contact.

"You have to admit, last night was really risky. I couldn't stop thinking about what would've happened if it had been Mr. Bannister who walked in on us."

His smile spreads wider, revealing perfectly white teeth and turning his expression seductive.

"I couldn't stop thinking about yesterday either, though none of my thoughts included Mr. Bannister."

I clutch the folio in my lap tighter.

"Mr. Park."

He sighs and his shoulders sink the tiniest bit. The rare, glorious smile is gone, replaced by his usual stoic expression.

"Very well, Ms. Sanchez. Back to business as usual."

He stands up to walk to his desk before turning.

"'Usual' means the cold shoulder act is done, too, right? Let's not let a few lapses in professionalism get in the way of our great working relationship."

Right. What every girl dreams of: a great *working* relationship with her super hot boss.

"Of course. I think we're even now."

He raises an eyebrow at my wording, and I just wink before heading out of his office. *A relationship (even a purely sexual one) might be off-limits, but some harmless flirting isn't breaking any rules, is it?* I hear his chuckle as I close the door behind me.

Back at my desk, I sit down with a wistful sigh. I know it's silly, but I'm actually disappointed he didn't fight back. I mean...just a little, at least. Continuing could have put both of our jobs in jeopardy, plus a partner and his paralegal is the second biggest cliché in the book, right behind a CEO and his secretary, but it was just so...*hot*. Way hotter than the K-dramas on Netflix. *If I can't have Henry, maybe his brother can hook me up with one of his dreamy clients?*

Before I can get too wrapped up in another impossible fantasy, Henry's next appointment strides down the hall toward his office. It's Naomi. I shouldn't hate her for her perfectly manicured nails, her designer clothes, or her runway-ready body, but if my balled up fists are any indication, I definitely do. And they have history? *Ugh!* I may be happy with my big and bold self, but that doesn't mean a part of me doesn't die inside each time a woman who meets America's stringent beauty standards gets the guy. I wish a guy could be original for a change.

To make matters worse, she's been nothing but courteous to me and a model client to Henry. She doesn't even have the decency to give me a flaw to latch onto and pick apart in my head each time I see her. Instead, I have to smile pleasantly and return her nodded greeting.

"Hello, Ms. Watanabe. Should I let Mr. Park know you've arrived?"

Her perfect hair falls perfectly around her shoulders like it's in slow-mo, and she gives me a genuine smile.

"Yes, thank you, Ms. Sanchez."

I form my lips into the semblance of a smile in return.

"Mr. Park?" I say through the intercom. "Ms. Watanabe is here for your nine o'clock."

"Thank you, Ms. Sanchez," he answers. I wince at being relegated back to my formal title before realizing that's what I asked for. *Damn you, Mila, and your prudent decisions!*

Naomi floats into Henry's office as he waves her in, shutting the door behind her. Behind *them*. God, I need a drink. Since it's not even noon, I head to the kitchen for a coffee instead.

"Hello, Henry. Thanks so much for meeting with me today."

Oh my God. He's left the intercom open! I immediately plant myself back at my desk and hit the mute button, my caffeine fix forgotten.

"Of course, Ms. Watanabe. I'm always available to discuss the case. How may I help you?"

I hear something that sounds like a snort.

"'How may I help you?' Is that the reception I get after it's taken me weeks to even get a meeting with you?"

I snatch the phone off speaker so I can hear without all the ambient noise. I *knew* I didn't trust this chick. It's about to go down!

"I'm not sure I follow. We met just last week to prep for the mediation."

"Yes, for the mediation, but what about us? *Are we really not going to talk about it?"*

Despite having my ear practically inside the receiver, there's only silence.

"What do you mean 'us'?"

"Really? Is that how you're going to play it?"

"I assure you, I am not playing. I am serving in the capacity as your lawyer. Anything further would be unethical and I would need to remove myself from your divorce proceedings."

"Whoa, hold on. Let's not be hasty. I'm not suggesting any-thing inappropriate. I merely thought we could acknowledge the elephant in the room. Like, 'Hey, remember me? Your friend and occasional hookup from law school? How are things?'"

Another silence. I can hear it's awkward even over the phone.

"Clearly, this isn't coming out right. I didn't mean to ambush you. I was just thinking that over a month with an elephant was long enough. I meant no offense. I'll see myself out."

There's a shuffling of chairs and then footsteps.

"Naomi, wait. It is great to see you. I only wish it weren't under these circumstances."

She lets out a small laugh.

"Yeah, me too. For our daughter's sake, I didn't want it to come to this, but it's been over ten years and it still hasn't clicked, you know?"

"'Clicked'?"

"Oh, come on, Henry. You and I both know Tanner's not really my type. We were just having a bit of fun. Then a condom broke and the next thing you know, my parents are pushing a wedding on me to smooth things over. Tanner's parents were thrilled."

Now I feel bad for her. I can't imagine being trapped in a marriage for a decade.

"I'm sorry, Naomi. I didn't realize the circumstances of your marriage. I promise to do my best to resolve things as quickly as possible, and in your favor."

I hear her feminine laugh faintly.

"You always were a standup guy, even if you're a lot more...formal than I remember. Clearly, I didn't know a good thing when I had it."

Henry clears his throat, and I hear what sounds like someone standing.

"Anyway, like I said. I just wanted to clear the air. I appreciate you still agreeing to represent me. Everyone says you're the best for these sorts of matters."

"Of course. Thank you for coming by. We'll be in touch ahead of the next mediation."

I hear footsteps and quickly hang up the phone. *Clear the air, my ass.* This bitch definitely wants Henry back. And I'm the idiot who just rolled out the red carpet for her to do it.

CHAPTER FOURTEEN

Henry

It's been hours, my last meeting has long since finished, and I'm still reeling from my conversation with Naomi. I assumed she sought me out as her attorney—if you want to stick it to your ex, I *am* the best. Now it seems she's had another agenda all along. The way she tossed in that she never loved Tanner? That she didn't know a good thing when she had it? What am I supposed to do with that? So far, the answer has been "obsess about it all day until the pages of your brief bleed together and you have no choice but to go home". I'm sure I'll obsess over it some more there, too.

My knight in shining armor instincts kicked into high gear at what sounded like a damsel in distress in my office. A damsel I know intimately, and after months of living like a monk. I almost reached out to hold her, complicated history be damned. Thank God I controlled myself. Taking on Naomi's case was already an ethical gray area; that meeting threatened to send me all the way to black.

All that was on the heels of Mila calling things off, which was...*fine*. I mean, I *did* masturbate furiously to her last night—and probably will again tonight—but she's right. I have rules for a reason, even if I seem to forget them every time she brushes past me and I catch her scent, or whenever she pouts those luscious lips when she disagrees with me but thinks I don't notice. It's taken all my energy to convince myself we would be nothing but a complete catastrophe.

I allow myself a ten second pity party over my day from hell, but look up in time to see Camila heading toward the elevator. I'm on my feet a moment later.

"Ms. Sanchez!" *Am I yelling? I'm not trying to scare her, for God's sake.* I take a quick breath and try to compose myself. "Are you heading out?" I ask in a much less desperate tone.

She scowls briefly before schooling her face into a neutral expression.

"Yes, sir. I have an engagement this evening."

I don't bother to hide my displeasure.

"I thought you said the cold shoulder treatment was over, Ms. Sanchez."

She looks at me confused and takes another step towards the elevators.

"Uh, it is, Mr. Park. I've had this commitment on your calendar since last week."

I come within touching distance of her, relieved she doesn't pull away.

"Really? I don't remember seeing anything."

She folds her arms, and that adorable pout is in full bloom.

"Yes. *Really.* And if I don't leave in the next ten minutes, I'll be late."

She turns to leave again, and I catch her arm by the elbow. I would worry I'd crossed a line if I didn't see her eyes dilate at my touch.

"Just a moment, Ms. Sanchez. I'll ride down with you."

She rolls her eyes but still waits as I grab my suitcase and lock my office door. I'm not getting anything done anyway.

We walk towards the elevator in silence, and I push the down button. I see her sneak a glance at me and hide my smirk. *Your words say "let's keep things professional", but your body clearly wants a repeat of last night, Camila.*

Too bad it looks like she's on her way to a date. I should have known. Today's velvet, indigo dress that catches the light and barely reaches mid-thigh has been doing a number on me all day. I follow her onto the empty elevator, sensing her nervousness as the doors close behind us.

"So...Hot date tonight?"

I miss "casual" by a mile and she rolls her midnight eyes at me again. Someone's earned a spanking.

"If you must know," she sighs irritably, "I have a meeting with my TA to go over some questions I had after the last exam."

"TA? Exam? Are you in school, Ms. Sanchez?"

She shifts uncomfortably, glancing at the numbers as they count down the floors.

"Y-Yes, actually."

I turn to face her, but she refuses to make eye contact.

"Well, Ms. Sanchez? Are you going to tell me what you're going to school for, or do I have to guess?"

She's worrying her bottom lip between her teeth now. Why wouldn't she want to tell me?

"I'm in l-law school actually," she admits hesitantly, her eyes still locked on the descending numbers.

I stare at her, mouth agape. A light breeze could knock me over, like the one from the elevator doors as they finally open. Camila dives out, eager for an escape. I recover just as the doors start to close, stopping them with my briefcase. She's already halfway across the lobby.

"Ms. Sanchez." She keeps walking. "Camila!" At her first name, she reluctantly turns around. I quietly savor the pleasure I know she gets from hearing her name on my lips.

"Do you want to tell me why you would hide the fact that you're in law school from your boss, who just so happens to be a partner at a law firm?"

Her eyes dart between me and the revolving doors of the lobby.

"Mr. Park, I really do need to get going. Office hours end at seven."

I walk ahead of her and gesture to my car waiting out front.

"Murray and I will give you a ride. You can't drop news like that and think I won't have follow-up questions."

Her shoulders slump in defeat as she heads towards the car. Murray opens the door and I scoot in behind her, doing my best not to notice the way her skirt rides up as she steps in.

Murray automatically raises the privacy screen once he has the address. I make a mental note to add another zero to his Christmas bonus and then turn to Camila, who's staring out the window.

"So, do you want to tell me why you've never mentioned you're in law school? What school? What year are you?"

She keeps her eyes on the passing city blocks as she answers me in a small voice.

"I'm doing the online program at Syracuse, and I'm in my last semester."

All the air whooshes out of my lungs as I fall back against my seat.

"Your *last semester*? You've kept the fact that you're going to law school a secret for *three years*?"

She smiles at me sheepishly.

"Five years, actually. The online program takes a bit more time when you have to juggle a full-time job."

I let out a humorless laugh.

"Wow. If I ever need an accomplice or help hiding a body, I'll keep you in mind. Your lips are sealed like Fort Knox."

Her smile drops at the thick sarcasm in my voice and she lays her small hand on my forearm. I'm too pissed to enjoy the contact.

"Mr. Park, are you...upset that I never told you I'm going to law school?"

Before I can answer, the car pulls to a stop. Murray's voice filters in through the intercom.

"We've arrived, Ms. Sanchez."

She gives me a worried look before silently stepping out of the car.

I keep telling myself it shouldn't hurt that she kept law school a secret. She's a grown woman, and what she does outside of work is not my concern. In fact, everyone at BBS&P knows I prefer it when they leave personal matters at home. But a paralegal deciding to go to law school is most definitely work-related.

I finger comb my hair for the hundredth time in frustration. Why would she keep that from me? All these years I could have helped her! At the very least, I could've accommodated her schedule a bit more.

The double doors of Syracuse University's Fisher Center open and her caramel leg steps out gracefully, followed shortly by the rest of her supple body. My anger and hurt completely evaporate at the sight of her. *How am I supposed to keep my hands off her when her curves shout "hands on" loud enough to make me sweat?*

I continue to track her movements, and she stops abruptly when she sees the car still waiting for her. I honestly don't know why I waited. *Yes, you do*, the primal man in me answers. He's been pissed ever since I cut things off the first time, but, unfortunately for him, he doesn't pay the bills around here.

Her trepidation is plain to see, and I step out to greet her.

"I know I didn't have to stay," I rush to explain, "but I was really hoping to continue our conversation."

She looks at me wearily, but thankfully still gets in the car.

"Where to, Ms. Sanchez?" Murray asks over the intercom.

Mila gives him the address of the Parkchester, and moments later, the car is in motion. She turns to face me.

"Look, Mr. Park—"

"Henry," I interrupt, placing my hand on top of hers in reassurance. It has nothing at all to do with wanting to touch her. She sighs and starts again.

"Look, *Henry*, I am sorry I kept law school a secret. I just didn't want you to think my work would suffer. I've been busting my ass to make sure that doesn't happen. I need this job." The pleading tone in her voice twists something inside me. *Does she think I'm about to fire her?* She anxiously grips and releases the strap of her purse.

"I also thought you had a rule about discussing anything personal at work."

She raises an accusatory eyebrow at me and I wince, upset my *completely reasonable* rules are making me sound like an asshole.

"First of all, there is no rule about personal conversations. I just don't allow personal *calls* at work." She looks at me with an expression that says she's not buying it, but I continue. "Fine, I'm not big on small talk, but Mila, getting your J.D. is way bigger than small talk."

She looks down at her hands, and I realize I've been idly stroking them with my thumb the whole time we've been talking. I quickly pull my hand back into my lap.

"So," I say, changing the subject. "Have you chosen a specialty?"

She hesitates. Our working relationship may be great, but clearly, our budding personal relationship lacks trust. I clench my fist to keep from touching her again and paste on my most comforting smile.

"It's OK if you're not interested in going into divorce law. It's not everyone's cup of tea."

She visibly relaxes, and I let out a breath I didn't realize I was holding.

"Honestly, I'm just focusing on passing the bar for now. After that, maybe...entertainment law? My sister's been working as an AD for a while and she's fantastic. She's even taken a few meetings with A24, though she hasn't landed a gig with them yet. It's going to happen any day, though."

The love she has for her sister is unmistakable, and I smile to myself. My brothers may be a pain in the ass 90% of the time, but family is everything to me.

"That sounds like my personal hell. Between the actors, musicians, producers, and directors, the small talk is end-less."

She gives me a rueful grin and shakes her head.

"'Hell is other people', huh?"

I hide my grin and turn to look out the window.

"Not in all cases."

My implication is clear, and the sexual tension rises around us once more. I smirk when I notice her press her thighs together and continue to fidget with her purse strap.

"Sorry to take you so far out of your way. Will this be your first time traveling north of Columbus Circle?"

I grab my chest in mock offense.

"Ms. Sanchez, how dare you! My mom's last four birthday cakes have been from Conti's Pastry Shoppe. We couldn't risk baking her anything ourselves after The Salty Butter-cream Disaster of 2019."

Her chest shakes with laughter, causing two of my favorite assets to jiggle enticingly. My eyes rake over her body and I'm past the point of caring if she sees me.

"First, that is hilarious, and you've gotta tell me the whole story sometime. Second, you should try Artuso Pastry Shop. Their black-and-white cookies are my go-to whenever I want to celebrate...or whenever I need a pick me up...or whenever I need a sugar fix. Basically, whenever I want." She motions up and down her body. "I rarely say no to sweets, if that's not obvious."

I'm not sure how to respond to that, but she doesn't seem to be talking down about herself, so I let it pass.

Well before I'm ready, the car pulls to a stop in front of the brick tenement building. Murray comes to her door and helps her out and I realize I'm clenching my jaw at the sight of his hand on her lower back, even though I'm sure it's not sexual. Murray has been happily married as long as I've been alive.

Not willing to be outdone, I jump out of the car and run around to meet her when she reaches the sidewalk. She raises an eyebrow in question.

"My mom would pinch my ear if I didn't walk you to your door." She looks at me doubtfully but doesn't protest when I follow her into the building. We step onto the elevator, along with two boys no older than twelve. They are wearing khakis and blazers with a school crest, hunched over a tablet the taller one is holding.

"Wow! You made an End portal in Survival mode? I've only ever made one in Creative mode."

"Do you know where the strongholds are?," the short one asks.

"I found one, but the Piglings took me out before I could place the Eyes of Ender."

Camila's chest is shaking with suppressed laughter again, and I bite my lips to avoid laughing, too. As soon as we step off the elevator, both of us break down.

"Did you have any idea what they were talking about?" I ask, happy she hasn't asked me to leave. She sighs.

"Unfortunately, yes. My younger brother is still very much into Minecraft, though he pretends he's too cool to play." She walks to a door at the end of the hall and I wordlessly follow her inside after she holds it open in invitation. Her apartment is very *her*. It's bright and colorful, with way too many throw pillows on the couch and large windows that let in the early spring sun. Bold and beautiful.

She gestures towards the kitchen.

"Do you want anything? I've got white wine, sparkling water, OJ. I might even have a beer in there, though I can't promise it's good. Gabe left it here the last time he was over."

I'm in Camila's apartment. I'm in Camila's apartment with her...*alone*. This feels both dangerous and inevitable, and I force my logic and rules to the back of my mind for once.

"I'll take a sparkling water. Thanks."

She nods and heads to the kitchen, stepping out of her heels along the way. The sight of such an intimate act has me following behind her without thinking. She bends down to look inside the fridge, and I step further into her personal space. I'm so close that I can smell her alluring scent again, a scent I will now associate with secrets and lust. She jumps when she turns to find me looming over her.

"Excuse me," she whispers, stepping around me to place my drink on the counter.

I don't want the fucking drink. All I want is her. I step closer and she steps back until she bumps into the counter behind her.

"Uh, what are you doing, Henry?"

I step even closer until our bodies are flush.

"I think you know."

Her eyes widen and her breath hitches.

"But what about keeping things professional? What about the rules?"

I duck down and nuzzle her neck, encouraged when she leans her head to the side, opening herself to me further.

"I'm having a hard time remembering them at the moment."

She shivers when I caress her neck with my nose, taking a deep inhale. *God, her smell is intoxicating!*

"Your rule since forever is 'no romance in the workplace'. Are you sure this is a good idea?"

My hands move from caging her in on the counter to grabbing her hips. I squeeze the soft flesh and feel myself harden in my pants. I press my body more firmly against her, letting her feel how much she turns me on.

"Pretty sure, yeah. Plus, you've already proven you can keep a secret. What's one more?"

The words are out before I can stop them, and I pull back to look into her eyes. I want this, but I will back off if she doesn't feel the same. A wave of relief overwhelms me when I see my lust mirrored in her face, her lids heavy. I nudge her legs apart and step between them. I reach down to caress the skin on the inside of her knee, and I feel victorious when goosebumps emerge.

"I'll take that as a yes."

I drag my fingers further up and to the inside of her thighs, and I'm rewarded with a sensual gasp that heats my blood further.

"You and these goddamn dresses have been driving me crazy for weeks. You knew what you were doing, didn't you?"

She bites her lips and spreads her legs wider, urging me to continue my upward quest.

"You deserved it, blowing me off like that. If you'd just—" she moans when I bite down on her neck, then lick the spot. "If you'd just let your bullshit rules go after that first night at The Commodore, we could've been...getting to know each other for weeks now."

I slide my hands up further still until they graze the edge of her panties. I'm relieved to find they're cotton; the old Camila is still in there, buried under seductive clothes and makeup.

"You'll learn that I prefer to take my time."

I tease the seam of her sex through her panties before slipping a finger beneath the flimsy fabric. She drops her hands from my shoulders to grip the counter, throwing her head back in a silent moan. I kiss along her neck and collarbone, venturing lower still to the generous cleavage revealed by this infuriating dress.

"Henry...*God*. Stay right there. Don't...move."

I smirk at how ravenous she is for me, and maintain my tight strokes of her clit. I feel her get wetter under my touch, and a corresponding wet spot begins to form on the front of my pants.

Still indulging in her cleavage, I use my teeth to pull down her dress and reveal the dark chocolate nipples that have been haunting me since last night. *She has breasts like this and seriously thought I would let her walk away?*

Her hips are unconsciously moving with my fingers, amplifying her pleasure along with my torture. From the slight tremble of her thighs against me, she's close.

"Henry, I'm going to...ah...I'm going to cum if you don't stop soon."

I smile against her skin and increase the pace of my fingers on her clit. She whimpers in response.

"That's the idea."

The trembling in her thighs gets stronger and I plunge two fingers into her aching pussy without warning. Her warm wetness grips my fingers and I press down strongly on her clit with my thumb, pushing her over the edge.

"Fuck, Henry! F-Fuck!"

She screams into my shoulder as her orgasm overtakes her and I have the sudden urge to beat my chest like a caveman. Her ecstasy is tantalizing, and I'm now painfully hard and leaking like a faucet.

Her breathing slows as she comes back down from her high. She lifts her head and looks up at me shyly. She gestures to my raging hard-on.

"Sorry to leave you hanging. I don't usually like to cum alone, but you caught me by surprise."

I shrug, happy to let my climax take a backseat in favor of her satisfaction. She reaches for my belt buckle.

"Here. Let me—" I take both her hands in mine and kiss her softly on the cheek.

"There's no need. Honestly, that was perfect."

She worries her lips between her teeth.

"You don't want me to...?"

I shake my head and give her hands a reassuring squeeze.

"I told you I like to take my time, Ms. Sanchez. Have a good evening."

I step away and head for the door, leaving her panting in her kitchen. Sure, I've got blue balls now, but I can tell from the feel of her, from the sound of her, from how she responded to my silent instructions, that she's worth the wait.

CHAPTER FIFTEEN

Henry

"Pay up, bro! I told you he'd slip up!"

Noah's face looks especially punchable as Cory begrudgingly hands him a $20 over the mac and cheese. Mom's outdone herself with this week's family dinner, opting for a soul food theme complete with mac and cheese, cornbread, green beans, fried catfish, and oxtails. Adam and his fiancée, Maya, are here, and, since she's African-American, Mom decided not to include fried chicken. I personally don't think there's anything inherently racist about fried chicken—anyone who pretends not to love it is lying through their teeth and hopefully Maya doesn't think she's marrying into a family of bigots—but Mom's always been thoughtful to a fault. Besides, making someone more comfortable is definitely worth missing out on one of my favorite foods.

"Boys, did you seriously bet on whether your brother would start dating his paralegal?"

Mom levels a stern look directly at Noah, who has the grace to hang his head.

"'Dating' wasn't exactly the word," Cory mumbles under his breath, and I elbow him hard enough to cause a coughing fit. Maya's eyes are twinkling at the exchange and she's wearing a small smile, but she says nothing. Cory is shameless as usual.

"I assumed Henry was too uptight to ever bend the rules. He's probably got starch in his boxers right now."

He rolls his eyes at my glare.

"And I—" Noah interrupts, "told Cory that if he'd seen Henry, Jr. and Camila together, he'd know that was a sucker's bet."

Mom continues to look horrified that her sons would make such an ungentlemanly bet and turns to Adam.

"What about you? Were you in on this ridiculous wager?"

Adam holds up his hands in surrender.

"Of course not, Mom. I respect women too much to make them the subject of such tawdry conversation."

"Womp womp," Cory mocks, throwing a small piece of his cornbread at Adam. Adam picks it up and eats it smugly.

"That's enough!" Dad roars, looking angrier than when he caught all of us out past curfew covered in glitter from the gentlemen's club. Everyone, even Maya, goes silent.

"Did I raise the kind of boys who would reduce a woman to a trivial bet?"

"No, sir," Noah and Cory answer, too ashamed to make eye contact.

"And you!" Dad points at me with his fork. "Didn't your mother and I make it clear that getting involved with your employee was a terrible idea?"

Mom interrupts before I can answer.

"Now Henry," Mom chides gently, "let's not assume the worst. Sure, some people take advantage of their positions of power, but do you really think Henry, Jr. would?"

Dad grumbles quietly but says nothing.

"And," Mom continues, "don't we know quite a few lawyers who have gotten involved with either their para-legals, or assistants, or other lawyers in the firm?" Mom's getting the mother of all Mother's Day gifts this year—pun intended. "John and Deborah just got *married* last year."

She wiggles her eyebrows at me, and I almost choke on my wine.

"Thank you, Mom," I cut in, "though we're a long way off from wedding bells. For now, we're just seeing where things go."

Mom frowns, and I know I've lost her support.

"'Seeing where things go'? Henry, Jr., I would've assumed you were serious about this woman if she was enough to make you cross the line."

I shift uncomfortably in my seat and Cory's face splits in a shit-eating grin.

"Uh oh. Sounds like the golden boy is finally in trouble."

Dad gives Cory a look that wipes that smile right off his face and Maya's lip quirks. I think there might be some bad blood between those two.

"*Anyway*," Adam says in a tone meant to change the subject, "it's T-minus 90 days until Maya and I tie the knot."

Noah is smiling again.

"I can't *wait* for the bachelor party, bro," Noah says, smiling like the Cheshire cat. "You will not regret making me your Head Best Man."

Adam rolls his eyes good-naturedly.

"Head Best Man, huh?" With four brothers, Adam decided against a best man to avoid any hurt feelings, but that hasn't stopped Noah from declaring himself king of the groomsmen. Considering how slammed things are at work, I'm happy to let him take the lead.

"You're damn—" Noah stops with Mom's warning look. "I mean *darn* right! There's going to be dancing, drinks, and, of course, loads of ladies."

Maya's expression turns unreadable and Adam puts his arm around her.

"Don't worry, baby. I won't let these knuckleheads get me into anything too crazy. I've already got the best girl at home."

Maya's shoulders relax, and she gives Adam a sweet kiss on the cheek.

"I trust you, babe. Besides," her smile turns wicked, "your bachelor party won't be half as wild as what Denise and Tiffany have planned for my bachelorette."

Something sounding suspiciously like a snort comes from Mom's side of the table.

"We're going somewhere called..." Maya taps her chin, thinking. "Hunk-O-Mania, I think? Tiffany got us seats right up front and Denise said she's bringing at least $500 in ones."

Next to me, Adam looks almost green, and Maya finally breaks into a fit of giggles.

"I'm just kidding, baby," she teases. She shakes him gently on the shoulders until he cracks a rueful grin. "You know strippers aren't my style. We're actually spending the day at the spa and then the girls have arranged a group baking class."

Adam's sigh of relief is audible and Mom hides a laugh behind her napkin.

"Once again, Maya proves she's the coolest soon-to-be sister-in-law," Noah says, raising his glass to start a toast. "To Adam and Maya!"

We all raise our glasses.

"To Adam and Maya!"

On the way back to Westchester, I think about what Mom said. The attraction between Camila and I is off the charts, but what do I really know about her? For Christ's sake, I just found out she's in law school last week. There's a chance this whole thing could end in tears and flames. I scowl at the unpleasant thought. It might be ill-advised, but there must be *something* about Camila that made me take the risk. When I'm with her, I'm not *Sub Zero*, I'm just *Henry*. I think that's worth exploring.

One thing I can't get behind, though, is Mom's marriage mania. A healthy skepticism of all things marriage comes with the territory when you're a divorce attorney. I haven't been in anything resembling a relationship since...was it Naomi? Was she really the last woman I let myself get close to? And now she's hoping for something more as my client...

I sigh in frustration. I've had reason to be gun shy about getting serious. Naomi stomped on my heart and since that day, I've only seen more evidence that marriage leads to misery. Mom and Dad, as always, are the exception that proves the rule. I won't say anything to ruin Adam's big day—he clearly loves Maya—but I'm glad Camila and I are just keeping things casual.

CHAPTER SIXTEEN

Camila

"Oh my God. I think I just came in my mouth!" Rory raves around a mouth full of Eggs Benedict. With her eyes closed in ecstasy, she misses my cringe. A24 finally booked her for an AD gig on their next feature film, and I'm treating her to brunch at Bea. It's cozy, and the food is delicious; it's almost worth braving the Times Square crowds a few blocks over. I'm not sure the bottomless cocktails were a great idea, though, based on Rory's passionate gesticulation and current lack of filter.

I slouch down in my seat.

"Could you act like you've been somewhere with tablecloths, please? They're gonna kick us out!" I hiss.

She gives an exaggerated lick of her fork without breaking eye contact, and I gulp down the last of my mimosa to soften my embarrassment. The waitress swoops in like a hawk.

"Another round of mimosas coming right up, ladies!" she practically sings. Great. Just what Rory needs: more alcohol. Before I can stop her (or suggest water instead), the waitress takes the empty carafe and departs as quickly as she arrived.

"Take your time!" Rory calls after her, a bit too loud.

I like to take my time, Ms. Sanchez.

Henry's words have been echoing in my head since he left me in a quivering pile of need propped up against my kitchen counter.

When I got stuck in a long line at the grocery store the next day: *I like to take my time, Ms. Sanchez.*

When I set the timer on my crock pot for this week's meal prep: *I like to take my time, Ms. Sanchez.*

Hell, even when I got stuck underground in the subway on the way here: *I like to take my time, Ms. Sanchez.*

One second, I'm a normal, functioning adult, and the next, I'm trying to hide the response in my panties from just the memory of his voice. I attempt to discreetly shift in my seat, but, of course, Rory doesn't miss a thing.

"What's up with you, sis?" she asks, looking pointedly at my lap. *Busted.*

"Nothing. Just...used the wrong fabric softener, I think." I stuff a bite of waffles into my mouth, hoping she'll let it drop. She doesn't even blink.

"You've been staring into space every few minutes, smiling when you think I don't notice. And now you're fidgeting in your seat like you're in heat. Try again."

Shit. And here I thought I was being stealthy. I've never been like her; she'll share the juicy details down to the color of the guy's underwear. *How do I dish about sex with a sister I helped raise?*

"Well..."

The waitress thankfully arrives with a fresh carafe of mimosas and I stall further by pouring us each a glass. She downs half of hers at once, then puts her elbows on the table and rests her chin in her hands.

"Mmm. Thank you. Now spill it."

Even tipsy, she's like a pit bull. I push my food around on my plate, refusing to make eye contact.

"Well, I...sorta...hooked up with Henry the other night."

She raises an eyebrow in question.

"My boss? You met him at The Commodore a while ago?"

The grin she gives me is so big and knowing my cheeks flush scarlet.

"Oh really?!! And you seriously weren't going to tell me this?"

I shrug, suddenly finding the drink menu fascinating.

"Wow. I'm hurt, sis. So what are we talking? Over the clothes? *Under* the clothes? Under the *sheets*?"

She waggles her eyebrows suggestively and I can't help but giggle.

"Stop! I'm not telling you that!"

"Either you tell me now, or I stand up and sing a rendition of 'Uptown Funk' for the whole restaurant. You know I'll do it."

When I hesitate, she starts to scoot her chair out and I panic.

"OK! OK! Stop!"

She folds her arms but doesn't scoot her chair back in, letting me know she's not bluffing. *Fuck.*

"Ugh, fine! It was just a little...*hand stuff.*"

"*Hand stuff,* huh?" She scoots back in and takes another sip of her drink.

"Over or under the clothes?"

I slouch further down into my chair, trying to become invisible. It feels like everyone is listening in to our conversation.

"Under."

"Ooh!" Her eyes light up like when I used to surprise her with a trip to Sephora on break from school. *God, this is mortifying. I've got to get some female friends.*

"That sounds hot. Was it hot?"

There's no point in lying now.

"It was beyond hot."

She chuckles, and the waitress clears our plates. Rory puts her chin back in her hands and stares at me with mischief in her eyes.

"So, my big sis finally got some action. Thank God, because I was starting to worry."

"Lack of dick never killed anyone, Rory," I roll my eyes. "Why would you worry about me?" Now it's her turn to shrug.

"Ever since...well...*you know.* Ever since then, you've been great at taking care of Gabe and I, but not so great at taking care of yourself. First you started dressing like a nun, and then lately, you started *acting* like one. All work and no play makes Jill a dull girl, Camila."

For a moment, I'm too stunned to speak. Rory was really worried about me?

"Wow. I thought I had my shit together, and now my little sister thinks I'm about to pull a Jack Torrance."

She grabs my hand across the table and squeezes.

"You *have* your shit together. You have a great job, a great apartment, and you're about to become a lawyer so we can take Hollywood by storm." Her face turns serious. "But you haven't been having any fun." She smiles again, warmer this time. "From the look of it, you're having fun now. That's all I'm saying."

I squeeze her hand back and chug my drink, slamming the empty glass down on the table.

"You're right. It's past time for the return of Fun Mila!"

"So, Mr. Park," I ask, sitting so close at the conference table our thighs touch, "now that you know I'm in law school, does that mean you'll help me study for the bar?" I bat my eyelashes at him, enjoying seeing him sweat.

In the week since our night at my place and my eye-opening brunch with Rory, Fun Mila has been out in full effect. Every now and then, I call him Henry in the office just to see him squirm. I've been touching him unnecessarily—a hand on his shoulder when I give him a file, a graze of my breasts as I pass him in the kitchen—and slipping notes in with the papers on his desk.

> *Those new pants make your ass look great. ;-)*

> *I think about our after-work rendezvous every time I pass my kitchen.*

> *Are you up for some "overtime" at my place tonight?*

It's *definitely* against BBS&P policy but also unbelievably sexy to see his jaw clench, or the color rise in his cheeks, or the slight tremor in his hands when he finds one of my naughty notes. I've made it my mission to make Mr. "I Like to Take My Time" lose his cool and just take me. From the heat in his eyes right now, he won't last much longer.

"Ms. Sanchez. What are you doing to me?"

His voice is pained, and he's nearly salivating when his gaze lands on my nipples that are blatantly poking through my thin silk camisole. *Oh no! Did I forget to wear a bra today? I guess I shouldn't have taken off my blazer after that last meeting.*

I play coy, sliding the toe of my heel against his shin.

"What do you mean? I'm merely asking if, as a partner at a prestigious law firm, you would be interested in helping your employee prepare for the bar exam."

He pushes his fingers through his hair in frustration before grabbing my knee beneath the desk.

"Camila," he growls, "we can't do this at work."

"Do what?" I ask, eyes innocent while my heel slides further up his pant leg.

It obviously takes all his willpower to push my foot down and scoot away.

"Fuck. You know what. The notes. The touches. The fucking innuendos. How am I supposed to get any work done with you prancing around with your tits in my face, practically sitting in my lap?"

My smile turns wicked and I lean in, taking up the space he tried to put between us.

"You're not. Did you think you were going to come to my place, put your hands in my panties, give me the best orgasm I've had in months, and I wouldn't attack you?"

He looks nervously around for witnesses, but the opaque windows of the conference room ensure our privacy.

"Ms. Sanchez—"

"Camila," I interrupt, putting both of my hands on both of his knees, letting his masculine scent envelop me.

"Camila," he says through clenched teeth, "I can't do this with you in the office."

"No? Then where can we do it?" I ask, leaning back to openly ogle him. I'm happy to see a prominent bulge tenting his pants.

"At your place. At my place. Anywhere but here."

"Ooh! I can think of a few places right now. And you'll help me study?" I press. As a soon-to-be lawyer, I'd prefer to get it in writing, but this will have to do.

"Yes. I'll help you study. Just please," he takes a deep breath. "Mercy."

I grin as I stand, gathering my things to head back to my desk.

"Of course, Mr. Park. I really appreciate you taking an interest in my education."

I exit the conference room, adding extra sway to my hips since I know he's watching. He's been in charge far too long and he should know that won't be the case in the bedroom.

Alone in my apartment again, we do actually study. I may want to jump his bones, but I'm not stupid; help from a partner at BBS&P is invaluable.

While he's exacting and domineering at work, he's a surprisingly accommodating teacher. He patiently explains legal concepts that have been tripping me up for years, breaking things down in a way professors often fail to do in a virtual class.

Because he's a closet dork, he still has his study materials from his days at Yale, and promised to bring them the next time we meet up. He even offers to put together some practice questions he says will help get me thinking like a lawyer, not just a law student.

Still, concentration has been a challenge. First, he took off his jacket, leaning back to get comfortable on my tiny IKEA couch. Then he loosened his tie and unbuttoned his collar when we got to the multiple-choice questions. When the Chinese food delivery arrived, his tie was gone and his shirtsleeves were rolled up, revealing forearms corded with muscle. When he had to repeat an essay prompt a third time, he looked at me with a smirk, and I realized he'd been doing it all on purpose.

"You're not playing fair, Henry," I pout, reaching for the last crab rangoon.

He chuckles and takes a big drink of his bottled water. I shamelessly gulp down my sugary soda.

"Fair? Was it fair to send me all those notes about my ass and working overtime?"

I playfully punch his arm, annoyed he's right. I can hardly to stay mad with someone who sets my panties on fire with just the sound of his voice.

"Maybe I should say I'm sorry," I say, scooting closer to him on the couch, "but I'm not. You were such a tease the other night, and I wanted—" I gather my books and place them on the coffee table. "No, I *needed* to make you pay for leaving me hanging like that."

"Leaving *you* hanging?" He lifts an eyebrow, the smirk still in place. "I'm pretty sure I'm the one who left that night unfulfilled."

I kneel on the floor and revel in the eagerness on his face when he sees me settle between his thighs.

"I may have cum, but I was far from fulfilled. That was just foreplay."

I run my nails down his legs before reaching for his belt. His breath catches and he bites his lip. I love a man who knows when to shut the fuck up.

The fine leather slides easily through the loops of his pants, and I reach for his fly next, the sound of the metal teeth the only noise in the apartment. His cock pushes against the fabric of his boxer briefs, impatient for my attention, but Henry stays silent.

"No objections, counselor? I know how much you like to take your time."

He swallows audibly, and I can't help but smile at my power over him.

"No objections," he croaks.

With the green light, I reach one hand into his slacks, squeezing his length through his underwear. He sucks in a breath when I lazily stroke it, feeling it harden further.

More than ready to get my hands on the thick rod between his legs, I lift the material and his cock springs free, the force so strong that it almost slaps his stomach.

"Impressive," I murmur, leaning closer to smell the musk of his arousal.

His pupils are blown wide as he watches me intently. He's clearly as pent up as I am, and I'm happy to provide some relief.

I lean closer still, rubbing my cheek against the velvet skin of his manhood. I give the tip a small peck, enjoying the salty pearl of precum that coats my lips, and open my mouth to engulf his head in a full, wet kiss.

"Goddamn, Mila," he hisses, his hands clutching the fabric of my couch. *Pretty good, but I can tell he's still holding back.*

I take more of his cock into my mouth, swirling my tongue around to feel all the ridges of his girth. God, this is going to feel amazing when it's inside me.

His breath is coming in pants, but a loud moan escapes when I use one hand to caress and squeeze the flesh of his sac. He curses violently and pushes himself further into my mouth, knocking against my tonsils. *That's more like it.*

I continue to massage his balls with one hand, stroking the portion of his dick I can't fit into my mouth with the other. He starts bucking uncontrollably, muttering filthy half sentences that make me grow wetter, burn hotter.

"Fuck yes."

"Oh my...ah!"

"Wait, ugh, mmm."

Am I going to cum just from sucking Henry's cock? That would be a first, but it feels possible, given the desperate clenching of my pussy.

"Holy fuck!" he shouts, as his warm cum fills my mouth. I continue to stroke and suck his dick, coaxing the evidence of his pleasure up from his balls and down his shaft to get every. Last. Drop. I didn't fall over the edge with him, but I'm out of breath, and my thighs are wet with my own excitement. Henry, likewise, is panting, trying—and failing—to keep his cool.

"Camila, that was..." he gestures, searching for words before dropping his hand with a slap on his thigh, completely dumfounded. I preen at the implied compliment.

"Yes, it was."

I sit back on my feet and gasp when Henry abruptly pulls me up to sit next to him on the couch.

"Let's get one thing straight, Camila. I want this. I want *you*."

"I want you too," I whisper, leaning into his hard body.

"But," he continues, "we have to keep this quiet around the office. No more little notes, no special looks. At work, I'm just Henry Park, Jr., your boss. Whatever happens between us *after* work stays between us."

He looks at me, still breathing hard, but with an expression that begs me to take him seriously.

"It stays between us. Of course," I nod.

He gives me a quick, hard kiss on the lips, then groans. I follow his eyes to the clock on the wall. 12:37 AM.

"That was amazing, and I'd love to continue, but..."

"But it's late," I finish. He nods grimly and starts pulling his pants up, looking around for his tie.

He gives me another sweet kiss on his way out the door, and I lean my head against it once it's closed. Henry is so much better than even my dirtiest fantasies. I'm in so much fucking trouble.

CHAPTER SEVENTEEN

Henry

"Why, oh why, do our younger brothers still insist on these flag football games?" Noah huffs, trailing behind Adam (the baby) as he sails into the end zone, flags intact.

I stop short next to him and pat him on the back with a smirk.

"Aw, what's wrong, Noah? Can't keep up? I thought I was the 'old man' and you were the younger twin."

As expected, Noah turns and chases me back to the benches on the sidelines, shouting expletives the whole way. I run backwards just to taunt him.

"Dick," he grumbles when he sits down, hitting me in the face with a sweat towel. *Yuck!* I hope to God it's just water on this towel.

The brothers have had a semi-regular game since Cory was in college and got really into intramurals. It was either this or ultimate frisbee. Noah may bitch, but I know it keeps all of us sane. We agreed to continue even while our middle brother, Damon, has been overseas playing professional basketball, but it's always better when we're all here.

Luckily, Damon will be home for Adam's wedding in a month or so and we will overload him with brotherly love a.k.a. drinking, partying, and gossiping like a bunch of teenage girls. With my schedule, I'm bound to miss some of it, but between the wedding and the off-season, I'll make sure Damon and I get some quality time together.

Cory waves his hands in front of my face from next to me on the bench.

"Earth to Henry! Are you in there, man?"

I take the bottle Adam hands me and empty it before answering.

"I'm here. Just looking forward to Damon coming home. These seasons feel like they're getting longer and longer."

Adam looks a bit sad—he's the closest with Damon—but shrugs it off before anyone else can see. Noah throws his arm around Adam's shoulders.

"Speaking of Damon coming home, are you excited about the big day?"

Adam's grinning from ear to ear now.

"Hell yeah. I can't wait to lock Maya down and pump a baby in her."

"Dude! Gross!" Cory yells with a full-body shiver. "Sex has one purpose and one purpose only: getting a nut."

I turn to Cory with a raised eyebrow.

"I don't think that's technically true, Cory."

Noah and Adam both burst out laughing, but Cory stands firm.

"It's bad enough two of my brothers are settling down. Whatever happened to the bachelor pact?"

Noah rolls his eyes.

"Do you mean the bachelor pact we made when you were in high school? *That* bachelor pact?"

"And who's the other brother settling down?" I interrupt. "As far as I know, Adam's the only one with a wedding coming up."

I turn to see Noah looking uncomfortable and Cory with his usual shit-eating grin.

"*You*, bro," Cory answers. "You and Sienna are well on your way."

"First of all, it's Camila." Cory snorts at my correction, like I've just proven his point. "Second of all, it's not serious. We're just hanging out a bit after work."

"*And* you're tutoring her for the bar exam," Cory adds, clearly enjoying one of the few times he's had something to hold over me. "Noah filled me in. You went over to help her study and then she gave you an *oral report* for some extra credit." Cory makes an obscene gesture on the word "oral" to ensure I don't miss his meaning. I shoot daggers at Noah who at least has the shame to hang his head.

"Dude!" I yell at Noah. "So much for twin code!"

"I didn't know it was a secret, bro," Noah pleads, clearly contrite. *That's the last time I share* anything *with him!*

"Are you sure you should be helping her study?" Cory asks. From the look on his face, I won't like what he says next. "I mean, the last time you helped a woman study, she jumped on your teammate's dick like a pogo stick."

The next few seconds are a blur. When I come to, Adam looks horrified, Cory's on the ground rubbing his jaw, and Noah has me by the shoulders, holding me back from pounding Cory into the dirt.

"Not cool, bro!" Noah yells at Cory. A bruise is already forming on Cory's face.

"Why are you yelling at me?! *He* threw the first punch!" Cory whines.

"You fucking asked for it, man," Adam interjects. "Talking about Naomi is a low blow."

"You know what? Fuck you," I spit at Cory, still seeing red. If Noah weren't holding me, I would've kicked him in the ribs by now. "I don't need this and I don't need *you*." I shake Noah off roughly and head for my car.

"Get off me, man. And don't fuckin' call me the next time you want a legal review on a contract."

Adam hurries to put away his things, yelling after me, and Noah jogs to catch up. Just as I'm opening the car door, he grabs my arm.

"Hold up, bro!"

I yank my arm out of his grip and whirl to face him, chest to chest.

"Telling Cory about Camila and I was foul, Noah. He's been an even bigger douchebag than usual lately, and you know he couldn't wait to talk shit. But now I find out that everyone knows about Naomi too?!"

The look on Noah's face is tortured.

"I'm sorry, bro. I fucked up. Cor and I were watching the game and it slipped out."

"And Naomi?" I challenge, unwilling to forgive such a betrayal.

"Honestly, I don't even remember telling him. That was *years* ago."

"You're right. It *was* years ago. Except she's my fucking client *right now*!" I start pacing, still amped up from punching Cory. That asshole deserved it.

"I play my role as big brother, coming out for celebratory drinks, picking up for the 'Council of Bros' even when I'm swamped at work. I stay out of everyone's business, and today I find out, everyone's been laughing at me behind my back about how things went down with Naomi." Noah looks desperate.

"It wasn't like that, bro!" I step one foot into the car.

"You know what? Unless it's Sunday dinner, don't fuckin' talk to me, Noah. I can't believe you."

I ignore the stabbing in my chest and slam the door shut in Noah's face. He can play the victim all he wants, but he knows how much Naomi hurt me. Why the Hell would he need to blab to all the brothers? And now he's telling personal stuff about Camila, too? I need some time to think.

Murray pulls away from the curb without a word, and the car is silent until we hit the Hudson Parkway.

"I hate to see you boys fight, sir. Are you sure the relationship can't be fixed?"

I sigh and unclench my fist; I've left fingernail marks on my palm.

"I don't know, Murray. Cory's an asshole, so I know to take anything he says with a grain of salt. But Noah? Noah's more than my brother; he's my twin. We're supposed to be on the same wavelength. And for him to..."

I sigh, frustrated at the whole thing. I don't know if Camila's worth messing up things with my brothers, but I also can't be the only brother respecting the bond we have.

I push the button to raise the privacy screen and put on some calming music. Murray's known me a while and I value his opinion, but nothing is getting resolved tonight.

CHAPTER EIGHTEEN

Henry

After the fight with my brothers, I'm on edge and doing a shitty job of hiding it. Byron at Starbucks took one look at my face this morning and handed me my usual black coffee, cutting the usual chitchat. Later, when I told that little fuckboy, Jeremy, to stop loitering around Camila's desk a little too firmly, she took it upon herself to call and apologize on my behalf, giving me the side eye the whole time. Then, after I raised my voice at Avery, the firm's head receptionist, for leaving one of my clients on hold for too long, people started practically scurrying away whenever I walked past.

I look up to the sound of a knock on my doorframe. It's Mr. Bannister. I sneak a glance at my calendar to check whether we have a meeting. We don't. *Shit.*

"Mr. Park. A word." The steel in his tone leaves no room for argument. Before I can answer, he takes off down the hall, leaving me with no choice but to jump up and follow him like a child chasing after his mother.

He nods to his assistant—a cute redhead most people call Cici—before pushing open the double doors to enter his office. As usual, it's striking. Over the years, I've expensed enough office furniture to raise an eyebrow or two in Finance. But unless you want your clients to balk at your hourly rates, you have to not only provide premium service but *look* expensive too. My office is a cardboard box compared to Mr. Bannister's. Marble coffee tables. Multiple Eames chairs. Suede couches. Ivory book ends on every shelf. I suppose these are the perks of being the founding partner in a firm with revenue greater than some countries' GDP.

Mr. Bannister takes a seat behind his large mahogany desk while I take one of the two seats facing him. They're intentionally shorter than his chair—it's one of the oldest intimidation tactics in the book—and I feel even more like a little kid preparing to get scolded.

"At BBS&P," he begins with no preamble, "we not only pride ourselves on being the best, but on being professional and respectful. As one of the partners at this firm, you're expected to model our values to the other associates."

I attempt to maintain eye contact, since cowering to a lawyer is like blood in the water to a shark. If they think you're weak, there'll be a feeding frenzy.

"Yes, sir. I understand."

Mr. Bannister nods.

"Good. I am happy to hear I won't be receiving any more calls from employees complaining about a hostile work environment because of your poor attitude." He looks me in the eye sternly, and I try to swallow as quietly as possible now that my Adam's apple feels about the size of a golf ball. Not trusting my voice, I nod.

"You're one of my best and brightest, Henry." He sighs and his posture relaxes just a bit. "What's got Sub Zero ready to scorch the earth around this place?"

I pause, unsure how to answer. A partner should be above letting his family interfere with his performance at the office.

"There was...a minor incident at home. Nothing to worry about," I rush to add, "and it won't be an issue again."

"You know, Henry," he says, leaning forward, "you haven't taken any vacation days in..." he makes a show of checking his watch before leveling me with a pointed look, "seven years. If something personal requires your attention, you're more than welcome to take some time off."

My back goes stiff at the mention of time off. I know I work too much. I also know BBS&P literally has an award for top earners. Their stance on work-life balance is simple: work comes first, and anything that gets in the way of that (e.g., family, friends, the occasional roll in the hay) is a distraction that should be dealt with accordingly. Several lawyers who've taken all their vacation time ended up with fewer VIP clients and smaller bonuses. I clear my throat and look at Mr. Bannister directly.

"Thank you, sir. I will keep that in mind. For now, though, time off isn't necessary."

He considers me for a moment with a doubtful look before leaning back in his chair with a sigh.

"That's good to hear. Don't hesitate to take a few days if that changes."

I nod silently and stand to leave.

"Is there anything further, Mr. Bannister?" God, I hope not.

"That will be all," he says, swiveling his chair to the stack of files on the table behind his desk.

I leave his office, quietly shutting the door behind me. On the walk back to my desk, I make an effort to wipe the glower from my face and replace it with my usual neutral expression. As soon as I close the door to my office, Camila enters and closes it behind her before leaning her hip against my desk. She says nothing but lifts an eyebrow in question.

"I just got called to the carpet."

Camila purses her lips.

"Did it have anything to do with you being an insufferable ass all day today?"

"Ms. Sanchez," I say in warning. She rolls her eyes at my blustering and takes a seat in the chair across from mine. She pulls a manila file from behind her back and hands it to me, nearly jumping in her seat with excitement.

"I checked Mr. Moore's financials again like you suggested, focusing on the property. You were right. He transferred ownership of a Chicago apartment to his college-aged nephew, a

South Beach condo to his brother, supposedly as a wedding gift, and it looks like a Vermont house is now in his mother's name. None of these properties were included on the asset list from Ms. Watanabe's attorney in San Francisco, and all of these transfers happened in the last two years."

I jump out of my chair and run to Camila, pulling her up into a spin.

"Amazing work, Ms. Sanchez! I just knew there was something there." She laughs in my arms, pressing her soft, full breasts against my chest. I gently set her feet down on the floor before I get too excited.

"Thank you, sir," she says, with a smile that hints at the new dynamic between us. Thank goodness the door is closed. I clear my throat and move to sit behind my desk once more.

"Amazing enough to earn me another study session tonight?" she asks. Her deep brown eyes are full of sinful promise.

"Of course. Though, with work like this, you may not need as much help studying as you think you do."

She smiles again, and my mouth goes dry.

"I'm sure we'll figure out a way to pass the time."

Murray didn't bat an eye when Camila followed me into the car this evening. He simply closed the privacy screen and navigated us to her apartment. On the way there, I made a reminder to add yet another zero to his Christmas bonus. At this point, it might be easier just to sign my BBS&P bonus over to him directly, but he's well worth the cost.

Camila lets us into her apartment and kicks off her heels on the way to the kitchen. Once again, my pants tighten at witnessing the intimate act. To see her in her own space, a space that is so much like her—bright, colorful, distinctive—as she essentially undresses feels like being trusted with a secret: the real Camila.

Ms. Sanchez wears stilettos, while *Camila* prefers sensible heels, flats, or to walk barefoot. *Ms. Sanchez* wears her hair in an elegant French knot or loose curls that fall around her shoulders, while *Camila* pulls it up into a bun or a ponytail with a scrunchy and barrettes. *Ms. Sanchez* orders ribeye or sushi for lunch, while *Camila* makes mofongo and roast chicken from scratch. Camila is relaxed and approachable, but no less devastating. I kick myself once again for missing what was right in front of me for so long.

"Dinner was delicious," I say, trying my best not to lick the plate. She might give Mom a run for her money in the kitchen department. When she starts to rise, I put my hand on her knee to stop her.

"I was taught that whoever cooks doesn't touch the dishes." She leans back on the couch, putting her elbows behind her head for dramatic effect.

"Ooh! Well, you'll get no argument from me. Dishes are one of the reasons I don't cook more often." She takes a drink of her club soda. "That, and there's no time because I'm stuck working late for a super demanding boss."

When I turn to look at her, she's smiling mischievously.

"Am I really that bad?" I ask. I roll my shirtsleeves up to rinse each dish before loading the dishwasher.

She lets out a bark of laughter.

"Hell yes, you are." She chuckles at the sight of my frown. "But that's the kind of boss you want. Someone demanding. Someone who pushes you to be better. You never let me skip professional development opportunities, and now you're helping me study for the bar. All of that is way more important than getting out of work at six on the dot."

Done with the dishes, I wipe off my damp hands and make my way back to the couch to sit next to her.

"Speaking of which, what do you want to start with today? Do you want to try a couple essay prompts, or would you prefer to work on some of the multiple-choice questions tonight?"

As I reach into my bag for my old study materials, a feminine hand comes to rest on my knee. Camila's fingers make a trail of featherlight touches down my leg until she's mere inches from my growing bulge. I tear my gaze from her wandering digits to stare into her eyes.

"Camila?"

"We *could* study," she murmurs, lust written plainly on her face. "Or we could blow off a little steam to celebrate the break in the Moore-Watanabe petition."

She leans in closer, and her hand moves up another inch.

"What about your exam?" I ask, raising my knee unconsciously to help gravity nudge her hand even closer to my package. "Time management is the key to an effective study plan."

She leans so close that I feel her warm breath against my neck. She presses her words into my skin, branding me.

"Would one night off really derail my study plan?" She licks the ridge of my ear. "I want you so badly, Henry."

She arches her back like a cat in heat, grinding her lush curves into the hard planes of my body and awakening all of my senses. I hear the quiver in her voice. I smell the tang of her blooming arousal. I see the color rising in her cleavage, a faint sheen of sweat on her breasts. I feel the sharp points of her nipples scratching through the fabric of her blouse and my dress shirt. My mouth waters at the thought of tasting her.

"What about a compromise?" I pant, logic draining from my brain with every swipe of her hot tongue along my neck.

"A compromise?" she whispers, still lapping against the column of my throat. Her hand boldly cups my erection now, and I clench my teeth around a groan.

"Yes. For every correct answer, you get to remove one piece of my clothing."

She giggles, then bites down hard enough to leave a mark. I hiss, and she licks the wound to soothe it.

"And if I get it wrong?"

"If you get it wrong," I answer, "we study for fifteen minutes, distraction free."

She pulls away from my neck with a smirk.

"Do you mean to tell me I finally got certified hottie Henry Park, Jr. alone, I'm giving him full consent to have his way with me, and all he wants to do is study?"

I take her hand from my crotch, bring it towards my mouth, and lick the seam between her index and middle fingers. Her eyes close at the sensual contact and I know I've got her.

"I don't *only* want to study," I murmur. "Why can't we do both? Orgasms," I whisper, placing a kiss on the inside of her wrist, "*and* exam prep. You won't forget anything from our special sessions." I give her my hottest look and see her eyes dilate further. "I promise."

She gasps before catching herself, biting her lip. Ms. Sanchez likes to be in control, it seems. If she's good, I might let her. She sighs, looking longingly at my mouth and the hard-on straining my pants.

"Fine. Multiple-choice questions, please."

I smile—I always enjoy a decisive victory—and pull out the sample questions from my bag. I shuffle through to find one that might stump her.

"Is a trial court in the First Judicial Department required to follow a decision of the Appellate Division of the Third Judicial Department? A: No, unless the Court of Appeals has affirmed that decision. B: No, because decisions of intermediate appellate courts outside of the Judicial Department of a trial court are not binding on that trial court. C: Yes, unless the Court of Appeals has pronounced a contrary ruling, regardless of whether the First Judicial Department has ruled on the issue.

Or D: Yes, unless either the Court of Appeals or the Appellate Division in the First Judicial Department has pronounced a contrary ruling."

A wrinkle mars her smooth forehead before her mouth turns up in a smile.

"D?"

"Correct," I answer.

"Pants. Off," she orders, gesturing towards my stiff manhood. I suppress a chuckle as I undo my belt, open my pants, and push them until they're a pile around my ankles.

"Technically, that was two things, but I'll allow it."

She scoffs and waves her hand for me to proceed.

"OK. Next question. Which one of the following types of services is only available if service by personal delivery cannot be made with due diligence? Is it A: Deliver-and-mail service? B: Affix-and-mail service? C: Service on an individual's agent designated for service of process? Or D: Service on the Secretary of State as a designated agent?

Camila breaks out into a huge grin, and I preemptively start unbuttoning my shirt.

"It's B: Affix-and-mail service." She waggles her fingers at me. "That's right. Time to get rid of that starchy shirt and show me those muscles."

It's clear she wants me naked as quickly as possible, and I have no problem with that. I'm already down to just my undershirt, boxers, and socks. I shuffle through the deck for an even harder question.

"Let's see if I can trip you up with criminal law and proce-dure." I know that's a weak area for her. "Two brothers were fleeing from the scene of a bank robbery they committed when one of the brothers accidentally killed the other. May the surviving brother be convicted of felony murder? A: No, because the brother who was killed was a participant in the robbery. B: No, because the robbery was completed before the brother's death. C: No, because the killing was acciden-tal. Or D: Yes, because the death occurred during flight from the commission of a statutorily specified felony."

By the time I finish the question, she's silent, biting her lips in thought. I convince myself whistling the Jeopardy song would be a bad idea. Finally, she sighs.

"I'm probably wrong, but...is it A?"

My jaw drops. *She got it right!* It shouldn't surprise me, given our years together, but a question like that could stump even a seasoned attorney. Most people get confused and go with what they feel is right, rather than sticking to the letter of the law.

If she asks me to take off my boxers, the game's over already.

"I take it from your dumbfounded expression I actually got that right?" she asks hopefully. My expression is chagrined.

"Right again. I told you you're already more prepared than you think."

She rubs her hands together with glee before pointing to my undershirt, indicating I should take it off. She's biting her lip again, this time clearly enjoying my impromptu striptease. Once

I'm shirtless, she reaches a hand out to touch my abs and I grab her wrist.

"Ah ah ah, Ms. Sanchez. No fun until the game is done."

She pretends to pout around a barely controlled smile.

"A decedent died intestate last year leaving a net estate of $150,000. He was survived by his wife, his son, and one grandchild, the child of his predeceased daughter. The decedent's estate should be distributed: A: Entirely to the wife. B: $75,000 to the wife and $75,000 to the son. C: $50,000 each to the wife, son and grandchild. Or D: $100,000 to the wife, and $25,000 each for the son and grandchild."

Camila lets out a frustrated grunt.

"Ugh! I barely passed estate law. I'm toast."

I grab a legal pad from the coffee table and make a quick diagram.

"If you're ever stumped on an estate question, I find drawing a family tree is helpful."

She leans over to watch me, her chin resting on my shoulder. Everything in me is telling me to turn and kiss her; forget the bar exam and show her the bar in my boxers, ready to make her scream. *Focus, Henry!*

She reaches past me to add her own notes to my diagram and I know she's got it.

"The answer is D: $100,000 to the wife, and $25,000 to the son and the grandchild!"

"You got it!"

"Woo hoo!" she whoops, shaking with pure joy. Her happiness is contagious, and I pull her into a hug. Despite all the pressure from my family, I love the law. Seeing someone I care about share the same passion warms something deep inside my chest.

"Alright, counselor," she says from next to my ear. "Drop those drawers!"

She sits back to watch me as I stand and inch my boxers slowly down my legs. Her face is full of desire, which magnifies tenfold when my cock leaps out like a fleshy spear.

"Wow."

I almost laugh. I love a woman who's not afraid to say what she wants, to show me she wants me. If the look on her face were any hotter, my glasses would fog up.

"Well?" I say, standing naked before her. "You seem a little overdressed right about now."

She shakes her head to clear her daze and stands to face me.

"Of course."

Without hesitation, she takes the hem of her dress and pulls it over her head. The material catches on her hair, and the French knot from work tumbles free to release her beautiful espresso locks. Under her dress, she's wearing a matching bra and panties in sepia that accentuate the honey tone of her skin.

She's a true hourglass: full hips marbled with shimmering stretch marks, a defined waist, and ample breasts pushing against the lace of her bra. Her nipples are as erect as I am, begging to be touched, and my eyes wander down to notice the plump lips of her pussy visible through the thin fabric. I audibly gulp and she laughs at my eagerness. Before she can undo her bra, I replace her hands with my own on the clasp in between her shoulder blades.

"Please, allow me. I've been dying to see what's under all these sexy clothes you've been torturing me with. I'll be damned if you get to do all the unwrapping."

With a flick of my wrist, her bra is open and the straps fall down her arms. When it finally falls away, my mouth goes dry. Her breasts hang in enticing teardrops, each tipped with a large areola the color of milk chocolate.

"Incredible," I murmur.

I grab her roughly by the waist and pull her close enough to taste each nipple, the pebbled flesh scraping the roof of my mouth.

"God, Henry," she moans, but I barely hear her. Blood rushes in my ears. I am feverish in my need, the tip of my cock weeping precum that smears against her thigh in our embrace.

"I'm going to fucking *ruin* you, Camila. I'm going to kiss and lick every inch of you, and then I'm going to fuck you until you beg me to stop." My voice sounds foreign to my own ears. I've never been so ravenous.

With her nipple still in my mouth, I shove down her tiny panties and push her down on the couch. The aroma of her flower overwhelms me, growing stronger as I push her thighs open. Her pussy is gleaming, moisture running down her slit and already leaving a wet spot on the cushion.

Like a starved animal, I dive into her pussy. I nudge her clit with my nose, lick circles around her entrance, and nibble on her labia until her thighs tremble in my hands. If her moans and whimpers are any indication, she's enjoying herself as much as I am. I take her clit between my lips and push two fingers into her unexpectedly.

"Oh my God. Fuck. Ah!" she shouts. I curl my fingers against her G-spot and hum into her folds. My face is a mess, covered in the evidence of her arousal.

Her hips jerk uncontrollably in my hands, and I know she's close. I increase the speed of my fingers and suck more firmly on her pussy. Her pants turn into whines before she explodes, her climax forcing her to grind her pussy even further into my mouth. I lap it up as the tremors overtake her, impressed by the sheer volume of her screams. I hope no one calls in a noise complaint.

While she comes down from her first orgasm, I take the condom from my pants pocket on the floor and roll it over my length with shaking hands. I might actually die if I don't get inside her soon.

Sheathed and desperate to consume her, I cover her body with mine. She opens her legs to accommodate my hips. The wetness of her climax and the sweat on my body combine to make her inner thighs slick, offering no resistance when I push into her.

I guide my cock into her inch by inch until I'm fully seated and we both groan with relief.

"Fuck me, Henry. Make me cum again. I'm begging you."

"Don't say that," I grit out through clenched teeth. "You're so hot, and wet, and tight that I'm liable to embarrass myself if you add begging."

"I don't care," she answers, grinding her hips against mine in a circular motion. "We can always fuck again. We've got all night."

And there went the last of my control. At her open begging, her sweet promise of more orgasms to come, I begin thrusting into her, plunging in and out like the piston of a monstrous engine. There's no finesse, no subtlety, only the blind need pushing me to chase my own release. She arches her back to press those amazing breasts into my chest and squeezes my cock from the inside. It's over.

I drag my cock almost all the way out before thrusting into her to the hilt, my seed filling the condom in hot spurts. I shout into her neck, licking and biting any flesh I can reach. She's clenching around me, her tight pussy quivering with the telltale signs of her own orgasm.

"That...was ," she starts, sounding awestruck.

"Fucking amazing," I finish. She strokes my back as I come down and goosebumps rise on my skin.

Has sex ever been better than that?, I wonder, sleep beckoning to me like a siren into the tide. If I said yes, I'd be perjuring myself.

I jolt awake, fumbling for my phone out of habit. It's silent. An alarm didn't wake me. I look around, disoriented, but the world is blurry. I grope haphazardly and find my glasses under the coffee table, thankfully intact. A light blanket covers us. *Us.* Shaking off the remnants of sleep, I realize I'm snuggling against a warm, female body.

Camila. I slept with Camila. I *slept over* after sleeping with Camila. I *slept through the night* without my noise machine, my sleep mask, or my blackout curtains.

What the hell does that mean?

CHAPTER NINETEEN

Camila

"**S**hit," I hear Henry say.

I open my eyes just a crack, not quite ready to meet the day after a very...*energetic* sleepover. Henry and I are a beautiful tangle of soft and hard on my tiny couch. His shoulder nudges mine as he fumbles underneath the coffee table one-handed for his discarded boxers. *Is he trying not to wake me up? It's a little late to sneak out.*

He reaches further under the table and slips off the couch onto the floor with a heavy thump.

"Damnit!" Henry grumbles quietly. My apartment certainly isn't designed for someone Henry's size. The thought of Henry as a bull in a china shop nearly makes me giggle until I see the look on his face. It looks a little like...*panic*.

My heart sinks. I just had the best sex of my life, and probably all my future lives, and he's having morning after regret? I'm not some naïve twenty-something who thinks a couple or-gasms mean I should start picking out baby names. I know what this is. But I thought we were on the same page last night. Now it seems like we weren't even in the same book.

I join him in his search for underwear, finding my bra under a couch cushion and yanking it on. Maybe the sex wasn't as good for him as it was for me?...If so, his moans and general wildness told a different story. Maybe seeing me naked was a letdown? As confident as I am in my own skin, I've never seen Henry with anyone bigger than probably a size four.

"Sorry," I say flatly, trying and failing to keep my tone neutral. "You're probably eager to get back to Westchester. Do you need to use my bathroom to freshen up?"

Henry turns to me, confused.

"You...," I lift my hand before dropping it with a shrug. "You're just doing a great impression of the roadrunner run-ning from Wile E. Coyote right now. I assumed that meant—"

"No," he interrupts, taking both of my hands into his lap. They're inches from his naked dick. "I'm not running away. I *loved* what we did."

His earnest admission releases the tension at the back of my neck that threatened to become a migraine.

"It's just," he sighs, resuming his search for his clothes, "I forgot to set an alarm. My phone is dead, too. How late are we for work right now?"

I give him a soft smile.

"Henry. It's Saturday. There's no work today. At least not for us regular people."

He looks so relieved I almost laugh.

"Phew! When I woke up without my alarm, I started to panic."

"You're good," I say, running a soothing hand down his arm. "If you want, you can charge your phone for a bit before heading out."

He lets go of my hands and gives me a worried look.

"Heading out? Camila, are you kicking me out right now?"

I sputter, startled by his blunt question.

"No! I-I just thought that...You know. We're keeping it quiet around the office. We just slept together. I didn't expect you to spend the night. There's...no pressure to hang out."

A grin breaks out on his face, and he takes my hands again. He strokes my knuckles with his thumbs and I try not to shudder with pleasure.

"And if I *want* to stay?"

I will my heart to stop pounding in my chest before he hears it. Even so, my Kool-aid smile is likely giving me away.

"You're welcome to stay, but I think we both need that shower." I look around at my living room, which looks like it was hit by a tornado. "And I'll need to straighten up in here too."

His smile turns rueful and, not for the first time, I'm struck by all the new sides of Henry I'm discovering. Sub Zero is cold, calculating, precise, perfect. But when we're alone, Henry is passionate, bossy, even vulnerable. Despite the solely sexual nature of our relationship, I'm eager to learn more.

He drops my hands and stands up, his exposed cock directly in my line of sight.

"Well, if we're going to shower, I guess there's no sense finding my boxers." I laugh and try not to let him see my hungry reaction to his nudity.

"I can't argue with that logic."

He gestures for me to lead the way and we walk down the hall to my cramped bathroom, made even tighter by Henry's broad shoulders and imposing frame. He's ripped, but not in a bulky way, like maybe a swimmer. Crowded in such a small space, I can't help but stare. He must swim every day and punish his body with boiled chicken breast and kale. God knows I've never seen him eat a French fry.

The smirk on his face says he's caught me staring. My cheeks heat, but instead of teasing, he leans past me to turn on the shower, brushing as much of his skin against mine as he can. Not once did he break eye contact, and I gasp with the intensity of my desire.

"C'mon, Ms. Sanchez," he says, beckoning me into the miniscule stall. "I'll wash your back if you wash mine."

I giggle as I step into the shower, letting the hot water rinse away yesterday's makeup and hair product, as well as all evidence of Henry and I's...study break. I still feel the telltale soreness between my legs, though. He was so big. And impressively thick. Of course, I knew that from the way he tested the flexibility of my jaw the last time he was over, but feeling it inside me was something completely different. Even soft, he's impressive.

"My eyes are up here," he laughs, probably having felt my gaze on his cock. I look a little chagrined.

"Sorry. I'm not trying to objectify you." Henry laughs again and starts soaping his chest...with *my* loofah and *my* body wash. He's going to smell like me—vanilla and orange peel—all day today, and I'm trying my best not to let that turn me on.

"Not at all. Please. Objectify me." His eyes are smoldering. "Objectify me *all night long*."

That makes me laugh, like *really* laugh, at my robot boss growing a heart and using it to tell me corny jokes. He starts laughing too until I have to grab his shoulder to keep from slipping. The sound I let out as I almost wipe out is super embarrassing, but objectively hilarious, and both of us laugh even harder.

"You might want to invest in some anti-slip stickers," he says, still chuckling. I stick my tongue out at him and gesture for him to turn around so I can scrub his back. Fair is fair.

I drag the soapy loofah down his smooth, tan skin. There's no give at all; it's solid muscle. I make large circles of soap, steadily moving down the thick columns of his back until I reach the curve of his ass.

I'm not an ass woman. I may have glanced at one or two Mets players' butts, but I've honestly never put much thought into men's asses. But Henry's has made me a true believer, and I will spread his gospel far and wide.

"Everything OK back there?" he asks, humor thick in his voice.

I clear my throat. *How the fuck do I keep getting caught daydreaming about Henry?* I've never been like this with guys before. Has it been so long since I've had sex that I've become some blushing floozie?

"All good. Just...thinking about my to-dos for the day."

He looks over his shoulder and his face says that he knows I'm lying, but that he's willing to give me a break.

"Is the first item on the list 'fantasize about my boss's ass?'"

OK, I was wrong. His face really said that he knows I'm lying, and he *can't wait to tease me mercilessly.*

"OK, ok," I pout, turning away in embarrassment. He turns around to face me and then cups my jaw with a large hand. It practically covers the whole side of my face; no wonder he made me cum so quick that first night in my kitchen. Come to think of it, I don't normally cum from just fingers, so he might be some sort of sex wizard. *Orgasma fantastica!*

"You're not the only one fantasizing, Camila," he says, then kisses me with a serious look in his eyes. "And you're *definitely* not the only one looking."

There I go again, blushing like a sixteen-year-old girl with her first boyfriend. He puts his other hand on the other side of my jaw and kisses me softly. He doesn't eat my whole face like the last guy I hooked up with from Tinder. He doesn't ram his tongue down my throat like the one before that, from Bumble. His kiss is soft, it's slow, it's...sweet. And just like I was baptized into the Church of Gorgeous Men's Asses, I'm now a convert for sweet kisses, too.

It doesn't stay sweet, though. How could it, with such naked attraction between us and naked...bodies? Each kiss gets more urgent until teeth are biting necks, hands are gripping hips, and we begin sliding our bodies along each other's, as close as two people can get with a condom two rooms away. I press against him, moving up and down, enjoying the slickness from the soap still running off his body.

It's probably the wettest dry humping in history and most definitely the hottest. Our moans and groans fill the air already thick with steam. I'm rubbing my mound against his thigh as he thrusts his cock against my hip and it's so good and so...different. Different *good*. He's panting light puffs of air into my ear as we cling together, groping and grinding and chasing our hovering orgasms.

Mine hits first. My legs quake around his thigh and I shudder against his chest, using it to smother my screams. He's not far behind, grunting out his pleasure as white streams run down my legs into the drain.

"Have you ever done that before?" he asks, sounding just as out of breath and amazed as I feel.

"Never," I admit, and I bite my lip, worrying about the gravity of that.

Before I can analyze further, he shuffles me out of the shower and wraps me in a big, fluffy towel. Towels I splurged on with last year's bonus. They're Egyptian cotton, ultra-thin, and large enough to wrap around my voluptuous body.

He dries me off carefully, then rubs lotion over my limbs until I'm both relaxed and a little needy for him again. His care is a stark contrast to last night's frenzy; tenderness is yet another side of Henry Park. We dress in silence, sneaking looks and kisses, and I luckily find an unopened toothbrush he can use.

As I turn to lock the door behind us, I take a steadying breath. Spending the night with my boss was beyond my wildest fantasies. Spending the *day* with him might push my heart past the point of no return.

CHAPTER TWENTY

Camila

I come back to our tiny table with extra napkins and coffee creamer, only to find a huge bite taken out of my black-and-white cookie. I send Henry a playful glare when I sit down.

"Nuh uh! You did *not* just take a bite out of my cookie after talking shit all the way here!" He smiles sheepishly, blotting the chocolate smudge and crumbs from the corner of his mouth.

"You were taking too long," he whines, stealing yet another piece of my cookie before I can swat him away.

"Stop it!"

He breaks out in a laugh and I nearly swoon. He should be careful with that mouth of his. It's lethal.

"If you leave me with nothing but cannolis," I warn, "we're gonna fight." He laughs again at my empty threat, and I steal the sfogliatelle from his plate in retribution.

Last night was memorable, and today is already shaping up to be unforgettable. Since the weekend bus schedule is hit-or-miss and we didn't want to bug Murray, we took an Uber to Artuso Pastry Shop. Henry complained I was trying to kill him by making us go anywhere without getting caffeine first, then proceeded to put his head in my lap "for a quick nap". I didn't buy it for a second, especially when his nose nuzzled a little too close to the hem of my skirt as he "slept". Goosebumps spread across my skin and I pushed him off before the driver could scold us. He feigned drowsiness as he sat up, and it was clear from the look on his face that he had no regrets about copping a feel.

Henry takes another bite of stolen pastry and closes his eyes.

"I told you they were amazing," I say, not bothering to hide the smugness in my voice. He rolls his eyes, but still finishes my cookie, plus his own triple chocolate chip biscotti.

"So," he asks, a Cheshire Cat smile spreading across his face, "Where to next?"

"I chose breakfast. You can choose what's next."

Henry wiggles his fingers like a cartoon villain.

"Oooh! My choice?" He thinks for a moment while I finish the last of my cannoli.

"How about MoMa?"

I sink into my chair.

"Ugh. On a Saturday? That place is going to be packed, Henry." He tugs me out of my chair and throws our trash in the bin as he shepherds us towards the exit.

"C'mon, party pooper. It'll be fun."

I poke out my lip like a sullen child forced to eat my vegetables when I really want cake, but his enthusiasm is contagious and I'm grinning by the time a cab pulls up.

"Every Sunday. Not exceptions," he says, putting his hand on the small of my back to guide me around an influencer too oblivious to notice she's blocking the flow of traffic. It's crowded, as I expected, but Henry pulled his donor card out, smirking when the ushers let us skip the line. His constant touches and looks as we walk through the 1880s-1940s collection have me practically buzzing.

"That's impressive. Rory and Gabe and I try to get together regularly, but it's not every week. Rory and I sometimes walk the High Line when she's not on location.

"I feel like it's so easy for family—even close family—to drift apart when life gets hectic. Mom was really the glue of the family, and I tried to become that glue as much as I could when she died."

We're both silent, and Henry squeezes my hand. He doesn't offer empty condolences years too late. He just listens, letting the memories settle between us. We move from the *Six Sculptures* installation into an exhibit featuring Picasso's *Les Demoiselles d'Avignon*.

"Oh," I sigh. "I *love* Picasso. It's amazing how he could create entire figures from broken planes and shards of color. His style is completely unique and instantly recognizable."

Henry nods and leans close to whisper in my ear.

"I love how radical it was for the time. Did you know these women are based on sex workers in Barcelona's red-light district?" My eyes widen and he grins. "Yeah. It was so shocking Picasso didn't display it until nine years after it was completed."

Of course Henry's an art buff. As we move on to *A Cubist Salon*, I'm struck again by what a shame it is that no one at BBS&P knows *this* Henry. They only know the untouchable Sub Zero: successful, hot as sin, but cold as ice. *This* Henry is a family man and an art enthusiast, silly enough to steal your cookie and caring enough to pull you out of the way of oblivious passersby.

Ready for art that's a bit more modern, I guide us to the *Calligraphic Abstraction* exhibit one floor down. It's amazing how many different interpretations there are of infusing abstract art with systems of writing. My favorite is Erol Akyavas's "The Glory of the Kings", while Henry prefers Dorothy Dehner's "Encounter", which resembles totems made of symbols.

I make a point to see the *Domestic Disruption* and *Divided States of America* exhibits, and Henry lightens the mood by leading us to Mike Kelley's *Deodorized Central Mass with Satellites*, a collection of sculptures made entirely of plush toys. By the time we make it back to the first floor, our fingers are intertwined.

My stomach makes an embarrassing sound and Henry looks down at me, alarmed.

"Was that your stomach, Camila?" My cheeks redden.

"No." He looks at me doubtfully. "All right. Yes. But, in my defence, breakfast was like four hours ago and fighting the crowds really takes it out of you."

Henry looks at his watch and winces.

"Sorry. I must've lost track of time." He pulls me toward the door, almost tripping over a double stroller in the process. "Capital Grille isn't far from here. Let's get you fed."

We start down Sixth Avenue, weaving between Spider Man impersonators and the line of tourists wrapping around Magnolia Bakery.

"Henry," I call, trying to slow down his pace. "Isn't Capital Grille like $100 a person?" It's also where he's taken a few of his other lady friends, if I remember correctly. I hope he's not running his usual date playbook. Whatever's between us hardly feels usual.

"It's around that. But it's worth it. They've got the best steak in Midtown." I pull harder on his hand, until he stops and turns to me.

"I'm sure it's delicious, but I don't need all that. How about we just stop by Lil Zeus, grab a couple of pita sandwiches, and eat in Bryant Park? It's a beautiful day."

Henry searches my eyes and I try not to squirm. I doubt any of his other dates preferred a food truck over fine dining.

"It *is* a nice out...If that's what you want, sure. Let's do it."

We push past Radio City Music Hall and walk until the tiny blue cart appears on the corner. There's a line—of course there's a line; it's delicious!—but it moves quickly, and when we walk a few more blocks to Bryant Park, we luck out when a couple leaves their table right as we arrive.

"Jackpot," I say, and Henry helps me spread out our food on the small, iron table.

After our late afternoon lunch, we wander around Manhattan, laughing and people-watching until the sun gets low. Under the Climate Clock in Union Square, Henry turns and gives me a kiss, right in the middle of the sidewalk. Passersby grumble about the inconvenience, but I barely hear them over the pounding in my chest. The kiss is sweet, almost chaste, but his hands snake around my back, squeezing me tight against him, communicating more than words can. He wants me.

He steps back and sighs, looking resigned.

"What's wrong?" Henry kisses me again, and then pulls me across the crosswalk to sit on the Union Square steps.

"I don't want to go, but I have to get back to Westchester. Prep for the week, you know?"

I *do* know, but I'd be lying if I said I wasn't hoping he'd stay over again. I run my thumbs across the back of his hand.

"It's totally cool. I have to study tomorrow, anyway."

We lean into each other and watch the breakdancers take turns defying gravity in the chaos surrounding them. Even though it's mostly for the tourists, there's always magic in Union Square. Like you're in the best part of a romantic comedy, about to kiss the man of your dreams.

When Murray pulls up, I feel a strange sensation in my chest that I try to ignore. Something warm and fluttery. On paper, nothing's changed between us, but I can't help but notice how right it's felt, just talking and...*being* with Henry all day. He's tender, he's decent, he's funny, he's fiercely devoted to his family.

And I'm fucked.

CHAPTER TWENTY-ONE

Henry

Noah

Noah: C'mon, bro. How much longer are you going to keep ignoring me?

Noah: I said I was sorry!

Noah: I'm really REALLY sorry! That stuff about Camila just slipped out when we were playing pool and Cory just can't help being an asshole.

> **Noah:** Between you and me, I'm a little worried about him. Something happened with him and Maya (I don't know what), and now he's even douchey-er than normal.

> **Noah:** Is that a word? Douchey-er? That doesn't look right.

I shake my head at Noah's rapid-fire texts. He's been sending them nonstop. I had to silence my phone when I was out with Camila, which apparently he took as a sign to text *more*. I scroll through days of unanswered texts since our big blowout and can only sigh. I'm going to forgive him—we're family, after all—just...not yet. The sting of Cory's words, of Noah's betrayal of my confidence, is still fresh.

I put my phone face down on the desk and think of her for the hundredth time today. *Camila*. She's fierce and sweet and so fucking hot my mouth waters just thinking about her. It was so hard not to touch her when she came in this morning, remembering how easily her fingers intertwined with mine on our walk through the city. It felt good. It felt...right.

My penchant for casual affairs is well-known and I've never felt the need to apologize for it. All the women I was with knew it was transactional. Our assistants would sync our calendars, we'd meet for a nice meal, we'd fuck at my place or theirs, and, if our schedules lined up again, we'd do it again. No holding hands. No deep conversations. No one had ever even slept over.

The truth of that had hit me like a ton of bricks as we passed Bryant Park after lunch. Before Camila, I had *never* spent the night with a woman, not even Naomi. And not only had I spent the night, I'd *slept*. I thought back to that first night with Camila, the first time we kissed. I slept then, too. Though a fair amount of alcohol was involved, I think I always suspected it was more than that. Better to cut it off before things got too real. Of course, I couldn't even do that. My feelings for Camila—and there most definitely are feelings, *big* ones—were growing even then. Some part of my subconscious knew; it had just taken me a few extra weeks to figure it out.

When I realized, I didn't react. I kept walking, kept talking. Didn't let on that while it seemed we were both strolling down Sixth Avenue, I suddenly found myself in unknown territory. The usual rules no longer seem to apply. Maybe they never should have to begin with.

The beep of the intercom cuts into my reverie.

"Mr. Park?"

"Yes, Camila?" I answer, cursing myself for my informal greeting. I can't afford to get sloppy just because my heart's started to feel a little funny.

"Um," she falters. From the tremble in her voice, she noticed my slip, too. "Ms. Watanabe is in conference room C for your two o'clock. Would you like me to join you?"

I'd love for you to join me, but I'm this close to bending you over and having my way with you and I don't think the client would appreciate being billed for that.

"That won't be necessary," I say, opting for a response that doesn't make me sound like a Stage 5 Clinger. I swear if I were a cartoon, there'd be hearts in my eyes.

She shoots me a look as I pass her desk. I smile reassuringly, and she looks even more concerned. *Shit. I guess Sub Zero doesn't go around smiling at people.* I take a calming breath as I push through the conference room door. *Game face, Henry!*

"Hi there, Henry," Naomi purrs, standing to greet me.

There's no denying she's beautiful. Long legs, silky hair that flows down her back, almond eyes full of secrets, and a mouth stuck in a perpetual pout. She looks the same as she did the first time I saw her, just with deeper smile lines and a sophistication she never could have pulled off in grad school. While my mind replays memories of Camila's melodic laughter ringing in my ears, her small hands wrapped in mine, her teasing smile eager for my kiss, my traitorous body reacts to Naomi, straining to rekindle a connection cut short years ago.

I reach into my briefcase for the documents that reveal Tanner's hidden properties, leafing through manila folders and stapled papers before I find it. When I turn back, Naomi's right beside me, her hand inches from my shoulder. I shift away, looking from her outstretched hand to her face with a question in my eyes. She looks at me with a hopeful smile.

"Can't an old friend get a hug?"

I eye her warily, and she raises her hands in a placating gesture.

"OK. I get it. So what have you got for me?"

She sits in the chair next to me, our knees nearly touching, and I remain on alert. Something isn't right.

"Tanner has been lying to you, Ms. Watanabe. We found three properties that weren't declared among the assets."

Her face goes hard, and I continue.

"There's a house in Vermont, a Chicago apartment, and a condo in South Beach." Her jaw and fists are clenched.

"These properties were all transferred from Tanner's name within the last two years."

Finally she erupts, jumping out of her seat.

"That son of a bitch!" Fury gleams in her eyes. "Two years ago is when I caught that bastard cheating on me with one of his fitness instructors. We worked it out, for our daughter's sake, and I thought we got past it." She's pacing back and forth now, getting more and more agitated as she speaks.

"I didn't file because he cheated. I filed because I was *done*! Done with the counselors, and the failed attempts to spice things up in the bedroom, and all that other bullshit.

"Things got worse when he started prepping for the IPO, then I got the job offer, and it was like a sign. Now I find out that asshole was planning to screw me this whole time?!"

I pull out the chair next to me, urging her to sit. She ignores me, continuing to pace.

"I'm sorry to have to share such upsetting news." I say calmly. As freak-outs go, this one is actually pretty mild. "Unfortunately, this is quite common in divorce proceedings, but thanks to these documents, we have everything we need to make him pay."

Her shoulders drop, and she finally walks back to the conference table and collapses into her chair. She looks tired.

"It's just such a fucking cliché, you know? *Woman takes her cheating husband back for the sake of the kids only for him to jerk her around in the divorce."* She leans closer and puts her hand on my knee. "This would've never happened if *we'd* stayed together."

And before I realize what's happening, before I can regain some professional distance, her mouth is on mine. I'm frozen in shock as her hands rove over my body, slipping inside my suit jacket, her fingers tickling the back of my neck. Like a fool, I open my mouth to object, to tell her to stop, and she uses that moment to push her tongue inside.

My body is in turmoil. Here she is, a shining paragon of what could have been, what *should* have been, throwing herself at me with a desperation that's almost unsettling. In this moment, I'm her life raft in the turbulent storm of her divorce, and I can't help but feel...flattered. To feel *vindicated* that she's back in my arms, begging me to forgive her betrayal with each brush of her tongue. My arms reflexively slide around her waist, pulling her close enough to feel my inevitable reaction to her.

Our undeniable physical chemistry is on autopilot, drawing us together like magnets, but alarm bells blare loudly, cutting through the sexual haze. *What am I doing?* Henry Jr. *Jr.* is quick to forget how careless she was with us. How easy it was for her to cast us aside in favor of a certified douchebag. How she never apologized for breaking my young, stupid heart. *And what about Camila?*

This is wrong.

I untangle my arms from around Naomi's slight frame and step back forcefully. Naomi wobbles on her heels, grabbing the edge of the table for balance.

Thoughts and emotions buzz around my head like hornets. *I'll obviously have to report this to HR and the senior partners. VIP or not, hooking up with a client could cost me my license. I need to nip this in the bud. I also have to step down as Naomi's lawyer. Do I tell Camila? The kiss meant nothing. We're technically not together, but... Shit! This is a clusterfuck.*

Naomi's quiet panting draws my gaze, and I whirl to face her, my eyes burning with outrage.

"Why did you do that, Naomi?" I shout, thankful for the sound dampening in all the conference rooms. She flinches.

"I-I'm sorry, Henry." She straightens the hem of her skirt, looking sheepish. "I honestly don't know what came over me. You're here, helping me get rid of Tanner like I should have done all those years ago. I just thought..." She sighs, looking defeated. "I just got swept up in the moment, I guess."

I angrily rake my hands through my hair and scowl at her.

"There was no *moment*, Naomi. That kiss was not only inappropriate, it was unethical. I'll have to drop your case now."

She huffs out a breath, her acid tone slicing through me.

"Wow. You're acting like I attacked you. Like you didn't kiss me back. You were two seconds from unbuttoning my blouse!"

My palms are sweating. I was such a fool to take this case.

"Naomi," I croak, swallowing around the tightness in my throat. "This whole thing was a mistake. You know there can't be anything between us. I'm your attorney. I can't be anything more than that."

The fight drains from her face.

"You're right, of course," she says, her tone resigned. "I'm really sorry I put you in this position. Between moving cross country, the new job, and the divorce, I feel like I'm going crazy. And then *the one that got away* basically saves me from my scumbag husband... I guess that's another cliché. *Woman can't get over the guy who ghosted her*." She laughs humorlessly.

"Naomi," I say, confused, "am I the guy who ghosted you?"

She lets out an unladylike snort and rolls her eyes.

"One minute, we're hanging out all the time, studying, grabbing meals together. The next, you're not answering my calls, acting like a complete stranger. Yeah, I'd say you ghosted me." Sarcasm drips from every word.

I take off my glasses to pinch the bridge of my nose.

"Are you serious, Naomi? Is that your version of events?"

She looks shocked at the bitter edge in my voice.

"Well...Yes."

Years of resentment and unresolved heartbreak bubble to the surface, and I pound my fist on the table, sending papers in every direction.

"That's rich. That's really rich, Naomi. You're right. We *did* hang out all the time. We studied. We hooked up. We were basically a couple!" Thank God for frosted glass so the entire office doesn't see me lose my shit.

"I thought so too!" she cries, reaching for me. I yank my body away.

"Oh, yeah?" I shout, anger sour in my mouth. "Then why the fuck did I show up to study that day and find you fucking Tanner?! Tanner! My teammate!" Her face goes pale, which just makes me angrier.

"You didn't know I knew about that, did you? *I never loved him. You were such a catch',*" I mock, imitating her voice. "Well, you were just as bad as he was! I mean, shit, Naomi, I was fucking *in love* with you!"

The words hang in the air between us, and I will away angry tears.

"Henry," she whispers, eyes in her lap. "I...made a mistake. He was flirty, and he was always around, and I... We weren't exclusive, you know? I didn't realize you wanted that."

I slouch into my own chair. My eyes are unfocused, and I remember I'm not wearing my glasses. I put them on and feel my composure return.

"That's why I was there that day. I wanted to make things official."

A tiny whimper leaves her lips. I'm too drained to care.

"I can recommend an associate who'll do a great job completing your petition," I say, slipping back into lawyer mode. "I'll pass along all our work so you don't lose any time."

"Thank you," she murmurs. She rises to get her purse and smooths a nonexistent wrinkle from her jacket.

"I'm sorry," she whispers.

The door opens and closes with a muffled thud, and she's gone.

CHAPTER TWENTY-TWO

Camila

Henry charges down the hall and points at me on his way into his office.

"Camila, I need you. *Now*." His tone is too lethal to argue, or to point out he called me Camila where anyone could hear. I scurry into his office and quickly close the door behind us.

"Henry, what's wrong?" I've never seen him like this.

Instead of sitting at his desk, he walks to his sideboard and pours a generous glass of whiskey from the fine crystal decanter. In all the years I've worked for him, I've never seen him drink in his office. I assumed it was purely decorative.

"Naomi fuckin' kissed me is what's wrong," he growls, sinking down into a chair in his seating area.

"What?!" I gasp. I drop into a chair across from him, mouth agape. Henry nods.

"Yup! I told her about Tanner's hidden properties and she snapped. She said he made a fool out of her and even cheated on her before. Then she starts talking about how she wishes we'd stayed together and before I know what's happening, she stands up and kisses me."

So, Little Miss Lawyer Barbie thinks she can come in here and shoot her shot! She gets to waltz in here with her perfect hair, and her perfect body, and her perfect wardrobe and just pick up where things left off back in the day? I bite back all the colorful language running through my head and take a breath.

"Oh my God! I should have known she might pull something like this after her little, private meeting to 'talk about us'," I say, making air quotations with my hands. Henry looks at me, confused.

"You *heard* that?" I wince. *Busted*.

"You *may* have forgotten to turn the intercom off when she came that day. And I *may* have accidentally heard your entire conversation." I try for an innocent smile, but Henry frowns in response.

"So, how did she react when you pushed her off?" I ask, hoping for a subject change. Instead, Henry's frown deepens, and a knot settles in the pit of my stomach.

"I...may have...*very briefly* reciprocated the kiss." My shoulders slump, and he rushes to defend himself. "It was practically a reflex, Camila," he says pleadingly. "As soon as the shock wore off, I pushed her away. It didn't mean anything."

I can see the remorse in his face. He's truly sorry. I shouldn't be mad at him. We never made any promises to each other. *So why does my chest feel tight?*

I do my best to hide my disappointment and summon all my powers of professionalism.

"So...What does this mean? What's the protocol for this situation?"

Henry clearly wants to keep talking about the kiss, but he must be able to tell from my voice, from my rigid posture, that the topic is closed. He clears his throat and sets down his glass.

"First, I'll have to report what happened to the other partners and HR." He anxiously scratches the back of his neck. "Assuming they believe I wasn't the one to initiate the kiss, in light of our history, I'll be removed from the case. I don't know what happens after that."

I *hate* Naomi. No, he shouldn't have kissed her back, and I'll deal with my feelings about that at home over a pint of Ben & Jerry's, but he's not a creep. The other partners shouldn't punish him because a client crossed the line, even if she is basically his ex.

"You might have history with Naomi, but you told them about it before you even took the case. Everyone who knows you knows that you play by the rules. Why would you suddenly start breaking them now?"

Henry gives a small smile that doesn't reach his eyes.

"I hope you're right."

We sit in silence, and he takes a swig of his drink.

"Speaking of rule following..." I pause, reluctant to pour salt in a still bleeding wound. "Would now be a good time to tell the partners about what's happening between us? You know...to avoid any appearance of impropriety?"

Even saying *us* makes my shoulders tense. Our weekend together seemed like a turning point to *me*,—from something fun to something...more—but who says Henry feels the same? I mean, *shit*, he just kissed his ex!

Still, I know I'm right. He can't come clean about Naomi and still keep us a secret. Not if he wants the full trust of the senior partners.

His jaw is clenched, his brow is furrowed, and his fingers are tapping nervously on the rim of his glass. He looks the most uncomfortable I've even seen him, and my heart drops. It seems I *am* the only one who thinks there's something real between us.

"I'm not sure that's a good idea. It'll be hard enough convincing them a client kissed me. What are they going to think if I tell them I'm sleeping with my paralegal?"

Right. Because all we're doing is sleeping together.

"True, but aren't interoffice romances against the rules? Maybe not firm policy, but certainly *your* rules."

His face looks so pained. If each word from his lips weren't tearing into my heart, I might feel bad.

"You're right. Generally, I don't think relationships at work are a good idea."

"Generally?," I ask, my eyebrow lifted.

"Well, when I wrote the rules, I was talking more about, you know, full-fledged *relationships*. We might get there someday, but we're just having fun for now, right?"

Of course. Silly me. I don't know what I was thinking.

"And Camila, as soon as we tell them, they'll split us up. I'll have to get a new paralegal. We can't be together and work together." He pats my hand.

"We're such a great team. We should wait to announce anything until we're sure it'll be worth it."

I feel hollow; brittle and close to shattering. How could I have been so wrong? What I felt between us was electric, like something finally locking into place after years of tinkering. I thought we were ready to take the next step, and he's worried about someone else taking his dictation.

I keep my face neutral and stand with my back straight.

"I understand. You're probably right." Henry stands to meet me, uncertainty etched in his features.

"I was going to wait until later today to tell you, but I'll be taking a leave of absence to finish studying for the bar."

"Of course," he reassures me, though he doesn't smile.

"I had planned to give you three weeks' notice, but given what just happened, I think I should go now. Let the dust settle and then see where things are with us." I start towards the door and he grabs my hand.

"Camila. I wasn't saying... I still want to be with you."

I gently pull my hand from his and open the door.

"No, you're right. We weren't anything serious. There's no sense making things more complicated when the Naomi situation is about to blow up. You've got a conference call in," I look at my watch, "ten minutes. I'll let you get prepped and get the soonest available meeting with Bannister and Banks."

I pull the door closed on his protests and almost run into Vanessa. She must have been standing right outside the door. From the grim look on her face, she heard more than she should have.

"Is that how you took my job? You *slept* with him?"

I push past her to my desk.

"I don't know what you think you heard, but I worked for everything I got." She rolls her eyes.

"I always knew something was off. I'm gone for three weeks, come back and I'm out of a job?"

"Didn't you move to support Jonathan?"

"Don't remind me," she spits angrily. "You know I had to take a pay cut when I moved to him?"

"I didn't know that, actually."

"Well, I did. And now I find out you wormed your way into a spot with Sub Zero by sleeping with him?" She looks disgusted.

All these years, I never realized. I barely even thought about her. I guess when Jonathan started hating me, I should've assumed she would, too.

"You can think what you want, Vanessa. Henry asked me to stay on because you were doing shit work and I could tell when you were training me that I was going to take your job someday soon."

She steps back like I've slapped her, then a nasty smile stretches across her face.

"Oh really? Well, how did you even get Henry to sleep with you, huh? Everyone sees the kind of women he dates. Models. Executives. Why would he waste his time with a fat paralegal like you? Be serious."

I smile to myself at her callousness. I will not miss this place. I won't miss this place or anyone in it.

"You're right, Vanessa. I am a fat paralegal, soon-to-be fat *lawyer*. I didn't use my uncle or my college roommate to get my spot here. I fuckin' worked for it. And I *kept* working, going to law school while you were planning weddings and honeymoons and girls' trips to Spain. And as soon as I get my bar card, I will leave here and I will *never* have to see or even think of you again."

I leave her gaping and head to HR to fill out the necessary paperwork for my leave. There's nothing keeping me here now. Maybe there never was.

CHAPTER TWENTY-THREE

Henry

Since getting my bar card ten years ago, I've operated by a rigid set of rules.

- *Tardiness is unacceptable.*

- *Proper titles and formal greetings are a sign of respect.*

- *Wrinkles, stains, and messiness of any kind have no place in the office.*

- *No personal calls at the office.*

- *One month's notice is required for any time off from work.*

- *No romance in the workplace, whether with clients or colleagues.*

- *No heating seafood up in the office microwave.*

Today, I've broken nearly all of them.

Yesterday, after Camila left, I met with Mr. Banks and told him about Naomi's inappropriate remarks and behavior in our last two meetings.

"I'm sorry you were put in that position, Henry," he'd said, no hint of sympathy on his face, *"but I'm also surprised you weren't able to find an alternative to stepping down. The VIP rates are supposed to buy them a bit more leeway."*

To say Mr. Banks was upset when I removed myself from the Watanabe-Moore case would be a gross understatement. If he'd been a cartoon, smoke would have been coming out of his ears. I may be a partner, but as the latest addition to the firm's nameplate, I am not invincible.

"Ms. Watanabe came to us specifically for the P in BBS&P! That's you!" Mr. Banks had fumed.

His reaction was disappointing, but not surprising. I let him know that discovery was complete, that transcripts from all mediation sessions were filed, and that our settlement proposal was already updated to include Tanner's hidden properties. Jonathan would take the case, and I'd go from being insanely busy to just unreasonably busy.

"I hope, for your sake, there are no further issues with this case, and that Ms. Watanabe accepts Jonathan as your replacement. That's the only way you'll avoid a performance improvement plan."

Mr. Bannister then gave me his back with a swivel of his chair.

So I'm on razor thin ice. On razor thin ice and running ten minutes late (*Tardiness is unacceptable.*) to an introductory meeting with a new client. Without Camila, I was stuck at the office until after midnight preparing for this meeting. The first of many punishments for dumping a VIP case was that the senior partners gave me less than twenty-four hours to prep. I had to sleep on the couch in my office and my rumpled suit (*Wrinkles, stains, and messiness of any kind have no place at the office.*) makes that painfully obvious.

I would have been on time if I hadn't been trying, again, to reach Camila (*No romance in the workplace, whether with clients or colleagues.*). The number of times I've called her is embarrassing; I even called her from work (*No personal calls at the office.*). How could she just leave? Personal issues aside, she knows I have a hard time clicking with my paralegals. I certainly don't vibe with my current temp, Rick.

Rick is Mr. Banks's nephew and another punishment for "the Watanabe incident" as people around the office have started calling it. He showed up in a polo shirt rather than a suit (!), dropped a call from a judge I'd been waiting for all week after what was obviously a three-martini lunch, and then he insisted on leaving early to meet his fraternity brothers for a game of squash. He's terrible. What am I going to do, though? Mr. Banks has already chewed me out; I can't now complain that his nephew's a moron.

Even now, passing his desk—*Camila's* desk—I can see he's got Solitaire open instead of the most recent deposition. God, I might actually beg Camila to come back. Things just don't run without her. At the office, at least.

Your life *doesn't run without her*, an annoying voice whispers from somewhere in the back of my head. *Shut up, disembodied voice! I've got a new client to woo.* I take a deep breath—something I never used to need to summon Sub Zero—as I reach the conference room and push the door open.

Decked out in what I can only assume is a Diane Von Furstenburg (her latest campaign) abstract print dress, Kendra Gray is stunning. The vibrant colors of the fabric, the golden notes of her skin, and the fullness of her hips visible even in her seat remind me of Camila. That's the only explanation I have for what comes next.

"Kendra!" I call out with my hand outstretched. I paste a smile on my face, hoping to cover the faux pas of addressing her so informally (*Proper titles and formal greetings are a sign of respect.*). I mentally kick myself and try again.

"It's a pleasure to meet you, Ms. Gray. I'm a big fan of your work."

I'm not. I'd never even heard of her until yesterday afternoon, but she looked lovely in the DVF runway footage I reviewed with the rest of the documentation last night.

She quirks her eyebrow, the ghost of a smile on her fuchsia lips. I can guess what she's thinking. *"This guy is a partner? He's got the professionalism of a first year law clerk."* After a few awkward moments, she shakes my still outstretched hand with a manicured one of her own.

"I'm glad you finally decided to join me for our meeting, *Henry*," she says, emphasizing her use of my first name. "Do you make a habit of keeping potential clients waiting?"

I wince while shuffling the papers in my briefcase, and my smile turns apologetic.

"Please accept my apologies, Ms. Gray. I hope you won't take this as a reflection of BBS&P."

I take out the last of my files and face her. She still looks a bit ruffled, recrossing her legs to the other side, but she nods for me to continue.

"From what I can tell," I begin, trying my best to salvage what's left of my usual decorum, "this case is fairly straightforward. TMZ captured pictures of Mr. Andre Gibbs entering his hotel room in St. Maarten while kissing his backup singer, Ms. Julie Baker. No judge will require a trial for a case with such clear-cut evidence."

Kendra sighs and drums her nails on the table.

"Well," I can hear the irritation in her voice, "that *would* be the case except for the ironclad prenup I sent to your office this morning. Didn't you receive it? I spoke to a Mr. Rick Banks."

Partner's nephew or not, I am going to fucking kill that little shit. I shuffle my papers again, attempting to hide my surprise. Finding out new information when it's too late to do anything about it is the bane of every lawyer's existence. That's why we have whole teams of clerks, interns, junior associates, and, of course, paralegals working around the clock to ensure we know everything there is to know. Ms. Gray places her hand on the papers to stop my nervous rustling.

"Mr. Park, look. I don't know much about you—you were a recommendation from my agent—but I must say I'm surprised. I wouldn't guess a partner at BBS&P who's won 95% of his cases would show up late looking like he jogged several blocks to get here. Either you're an imposter and I'm being pranked, or you're having one of the worst days of your professional career."

"Bingo," I mutter.

"Care to get it out in the open so we can get this show on the road? I have a fitting downtown in two hours."

There is no universe where a lawyer would treat a potential client, especially a VIP, like some sort of pop psychologist to solve his personal problems. But she did *ask*, and I've already made a terrible first impression. Maybe it's time to retire Sub Zero and actually be myself.

She sees I'm conflicted and her face softens slightly.

"I know you don't know me from Adam, and that talking about whatever is bothering you must be extremely unusual, especially with a potential client. But I'm also a human. Let's hear it."

To my great surprise, I open my mouth and tell her all about my brother "Harold". How he's struggling to work with an old flame. How his long-time assistant is becoming something more. All about "Harold" and his assistant's beautiful night together. How he might lose her if he isn't honest about their relationship with his "managers.

It was unforgivably unprofessional, and I doubt she bought it was about "Harold" for a second, but it felt...good to actually talk about it. To lighten the load of everything that's happened by sharing it with someone. Usually, that "someone" would be Noah.

"I can tell *Harold*'s in love with *Mina* just from the way he talks about her," she says, a genuine smile on her face for the first time since the meeting started. Tension bunches my shoulders.

"'Love' is a strong word, Ms. Gray. I said he has *feelings* for her." Kendra rolls her eyes. "Anyway, now it's all messed up. She walked out, and she hasn't been answering his calls or texts."

God, I sound like I'm back in high school again. Kendra smiles even bigger.

"It sounds to me like she's looking for a grand gesture. To go from being his assistant to his..." she searches for your word, "...uh, fuck buddy, is one thing. I know firsthand that it can be fun to sneak around with someone at work. The secrets make it hotter." She sits back in her chair, thoughtful.

"But I also know firsthand how tough it can be to move from fuck buddies to *more* with someone at work. And if she's plus-sized like me, keeping things a secret might come across as being ashamed of her."

"First off," I protest, "I don't think Harold would call her an...F buddy."

As if saying "fuck" would make this conversation any more inappropriate than it already is. She gives me a pointed look.

"Were they meeting up to have sex?" she asks.

"Not *only* sex, but...yes," I answer begrudgingly.

"And they were keeping it a secret?"

"Of course. Interoffice relationships are strongly discouraged."

I can't keep the defensiveness out of my voice. She gives me a meaningful smile.

"It sounds like Harold and Mina were most definitely fuck buddies." She raises her hands when she notices me about to interject. "Which is *totally fine*! But if she's still a secret and Harold wants more, the relationship has to come out of hiding." She checks her watch and stands. "And his ex definitely needs to stay out of the picture."

I stand too, completely at a loss. I must be desperate to be considering relationship advice from a virtual stranger. This whole conversation is straight out of "The Twilight Zone".

"Already done," I answer. She nods approvingly and collects her purse and portfolio.

"So, I take it you'll be going with another firm?" I ask, a grimace stretching my lips.

She leans forward and air kisses both sides of my face.

"Let's reschedule. I told you your win record precedes you. Have someone set up another meeting but, next time, keep the personal stuff at home."

"Of course," I reply, shocked Ms. Gray could be so calm about this. "Thank you for being so understanding."

She waves it off like it's nothing for her lawyer to essentially have a nervous breakdown in an introductory meeting. I walk her to the elevators and, on the way back to my desk, I think about Camila.

Ms. Gray may have a point about a grand gesture, but going out on a limb for a woman I care about has never ended well. When Naomi thought I was going to make things official, she slept with someone else. We're better off letting things cool down. We'll talk then and Camila will understand. She always does.

CHAPTER TWENTY-FOUR

Camila

"Congratulations, grad!!" some drunk guy slurs into my ear as he hugs me around the shoulders and motions for the bartender to get me yet another shot of whiskey. I down it, wincing from the burn, and the bar cheers around me. Rory and Gabe insisted I wear my cap and gown to Bronx Alehouse for the free drinks, even though they've also been buying me a steady stream of Midori sours and tequila sunrises. I haven't been this drunk since...ever.

"You doing OK, sis?" asks Gabe, taking one of the shots in front of me.

I moan weakly in response, trying to slow down the room's violent spinning. All the faces around me are a blur. Rory eyes me with concern and tries to get the bartender's attention. He gives her a nod to order, still pouring someone else's pint.

"Hey, man. Can we get my sis some fries or something? She's not looking too hot." He looks me up and down before nodding and moving on to another customer. I make a cradle of my arms and rest my head against the bar. Rory rubs my back soothingly.

"Thank God," I moan, my voice barely audible above the noise of the bar. "I was worried you were going to get me another drink."

She smirks, but doesn't stop rubbing my back.

"I'm not a murderer. Gabe and I just wanted to make sure you had a great time."

Gabe pulls a face after taking a sip of my Midori sour. With all the shots, it's practically untouched.

"Ugh! That shit tastes like a melted snow cone!" He wipes his mouth with his sleeve.

"Uh, no one told you to drink that, Gabe," Rory laughs through her hand. He scoffs and takes another gulp from the green cocktail.

"I thought you said you didn't like it," I mutter, caught in an alcohol-induced vortex. *Deep breaths. I will not vomit in public.* Gabe just shrugs.

"Eh, free is free."

Rory and I both roll our eyes at him, but I slam mine shut halfway through, since it made "the spins" worse.

On the surface, this past week has been a celebration leading up to my graduation from law school. Instead of getting up at the butt crack of dawn for work, I got to sleep 'til ten, study until dinner, and then take myself to the girliest rom-coms playing in theaters. I gorged myself on popcorn and Jujyfruits, grabbed a scoop of ice cream (usually cookies n' cream), and then headed home for more studying until I fell asleep.

On Wednesday, I met Rory for a walk along the Highline. She told me about her job, and how she's crushing on the director. *He's a genius*, she said. I tried not to chime in with my freshly bitter feelings about workplace romances. She's smarter than me, anyway; she probably won't make my mistakes.

Then, on Friday, Rory surprised me with a graduation dinner at Jean-Georges, courtesy of her first check from A24. We had our pinkies out the whole meal, and she did her best not to giggle too loud when I gagged after tasting oysters for the first time. Why people pay market price for something with the consistency of a loogie, I'll never know. The rest of the food was amazing, though.

Then today, Gabe handed me a beautiful bouquet of roses, tulips, and sunflowers as soon as the graduation ceremony was over. I tried not to tear up at all the love my younger siblings were giving me this week, but it was impossible. We'd gone through so much since Mom died, and now I'm done with law school, Rory's a legit Hollywood Assistant Director and soon-to-be producer, and Gabe finished Fordham last year. He's still not sure what he wants to do, but he's got options. We're all OK.

Underneath all the love and celebrations, though, was a dull ache in my chest and a persistent sadness. *Henry*. God, what a bonehead move to fuck my boss. Jeremy in the mailroom, I could've handled. He was cute and doting, and there was never going to be anything serious between us. Dating him would've been like eating cotton candy: sweet until it faded into nothing.

Even before our first kiss, I knew Henry was going to be major. Substantial and meaningful, like my great grandmother's pernil recipe.

And incredibly *filling*. Every night this week, I've thought about him before grabbing my vibrator to distract myself from re-reading his texts.

Henry

Henry: You really just walked out? No discussion, no nothing?

Henry: I wasn't saying our thing isn't special. I'm just not ready to go public yet. Not with everything that's going on.

Henry: Shit. I don't mean I want to keep you a secret. I'm not ashamed to be seen with you or anything like that.

Henry: This isn't coming out right over text. Let's talk about this like adults.

Henry: Please

He called a few times too, but I never answered. I was too hurt. Naomi may have kissed him first, but he kissed her back. *She's* the one he'll tell the partners about, not me. Guys like him always end up with women like Naomi. I was fooling myself to think otherwise.

A plate of hot, golden fries magically appears in front of me and I muster up a smile for my sister.

"You're the best, Rory. I don't think this is going to save me from the world's worst hangover, though."

I take a fry and munch it, letting the salty goodness numb my feelings a little further. *How many more plates of these will it take to forget Henry completely?*

Gabe nudges me in the ribs from his seat beside me.

"What gives, Mila? I know you're drunk, but Rory and I can both tell there's something else going on."

"There's nothing," I lie. "I'm just worn out from school and studying." I pull them both into a drunken hug, wobbling a bit on my feet. "Thank you both for making my graduation week so awesome."

Gabe chucks me under the chin and helps lower me back to the barstool. He grabs a handful of fries as payment.

"Compared to everything you've done for us, this is nothing," he says. Rory squeezes my arm. Her usual sarcastic expression is now serious.

"I second that and then some. Thanks to you, we're all successful adults." She jerks her head in Gabe's direction. "Well, *most* of us." Gabe flips her off with a smile.

"But seriously, a thousand fancy dinners and flowers wouldn't be enough to make up for all you've done for us since Mom died. Now that we're all grown and done with school, you can become the kick-ass lawyer you were always meant to be."

Gabe wipes at his eyes and raises his glass.

"Here here!"

The surrounding bar patrons raise their drinks in solidarity.

I am dead. Clearly, ten shots and countless cocktails led to acute alcohol poisoning, and now I am in hell. There is no other explanation for the horrific symphony of blades and car horns in my head, and the vile taste of roadkill in my mouth. *Yuck*. I gingerly lift my head to see the time on my bedside clock and the symphony intensifies.

"Oh, ow!" I moan, before falling back onto my pillow. That hurt too. A hand with three brown pills appears above my face.

"Here," Rory demands, giving her hand a little shake. "Take this ibuprofen. You'll need it if you're going to function today."

I groan in protest, but manage to prop myself up to take the pills. Luckily, Rory's also got a full glass of water. I gulp it down like I've been wandering the Sahara for weeks.

"Mmm. Thank you, sis." I put the empty glass down and carefully scoot myself up until I'm all the way against the headboard. "Now, why do I have to function today?"

My sister looks at me like I'm crazy and waves her arm around my apartment.

"First, we're going to clean up this pigsty. I mean, *damn*, sis. I have never seen your place look this bad."

I smile sheepishly and fiddle with the edge of my comforter.

"And then?"

"And then," she continues, lowering her voice when I flinch in pain, "you're going to tell me what really has you moping around here like the Phantom of the Opera."

A laugh bubbles free from my parched lips. That glass of water barely scratched the surface.

"That is ridiculous, Rory. I told you, I'm just worn out from finishing the semester. Hell, from finishing my whole *degree*."

She sits down next to me on the bed and pats my hand like someone would pat the head of a small dog.

"Yes, I remember the bullshit you told us before, big sis. I was hoping to get the truth out of you last night, but instead, you demanded pancakes before promptly falling asleep in the Uber." She pokes me in the leg. "So spill."

I sigh heavily.

"Things with Henry got...complicated." I slouch down further into my sheets. Maybe if I burrow deep enough, she'll leave me alone. Without warning, the covers are yanked off, and I'm sitting fully dressed in yesterday's clothes.

"Go on, then. What happened?" Rory never was one to let things go.

"Well, we hooked up a few times. You know that part. Then he started helping me study for the bar. And then the last time he came over, one thing led to another and—"

"And you bumped uglies?!" Rory interrupts, her voice full of glee. I can't help but giggle.

"Yes, we had sex. And it was," I sigh dreamily. "...It was *really fucking good*. He even stayed over, and we spent the next day together, walking all over the city."

"That sounds like something straight out of the movies. So what happened?" Rory asked.

"His ex happened," I mutter. "She kept throwing herself at him and then she kissed him!" Rory gasps and I feel validated. *You're damn right.*

"Henry said it didn't mean anything, and maybe that's true, but when I said we should come clean about what we're doing so we definitely don't get in trouble, he said we should wait until we know it's 'worth it'. He's worried about losing me as a paralegal!"

I struggle not to choke on the last words. Rory frowns and pulls me into a tight hug.

"I'm so sorry, Mila. You're worth the risk, and if I ever see him again, I promise to castrate him." I smile, doing my best to ignore the cacophony still assaulting my head.

She smooths my hair, tucking loose strands behind my ear. Mom used to do that, and the memory has tears rolling down my cheeks.

"Did you try telling him how you feel?" she asks quietly. "Maybe he just needs to know you're all in before he takes the plunge." I shake my head.

"No. I left. Turned in my leave of absence form that same day."

Rory sits thoughtfully, still stroking my hair, before continuing.

"I definitely don't agree with what he said, but don't you think you should talk to him? You worked together for years, then you finally made it personal. There are bound to be a few hiccups while you figure out the new dynamic."

Maybe she has a point. But even still...

"It wouldn't work out, anyway. If not Naomi, it will be some other woman like that. I've been his paralegal for years, sis, and he never noticed me like that. I'm not some CEO or some high-powered lawyer."

"*Not yet,*" Rory insists, and I could kiss her. She might be the spokeswoman for tough love, but she's also my biggest cheerleader.

I tighten the hug until she starts to pull out of my grasp. Even with me, Rory's always had a limit on how "touchy feely" she's willing to get. I don't take it personally.

"Thanks, Ror. Maybe I will be some day. But me and Henry?" I fall back against the headboard and immediately regret it when my head starts pounding again. "I don't think that's going to happen. Let's just forget it, OK?" I drag myself off the bed and towards the kitchen. "C'mon. I'll make us some coffee so we can tackle this mess."

Rory follows me down the hall, grumbling.

"Like I said. This sounds exactly like a movie. When y'all get back together, don't forget that 'Aurora' makes a lovely name for a baby."

I throw a dish towel at her and grab the coffee beans from out of the fridge. As she picks up the remote to put on some cleaning music, my mouth tugs into a hopeful smile.

CHAPTER TWENTY-FIVE

Henry

A week without Camila, and I'm beginning to think I made the wrong choice. I miss her. Not just her professional contributions, although Rick continues to invent new ways to disappoint me. Not just her body, although I feel her phantom touch every night in bed. I miss *her*. The woman who busts my balls daily, but also pushes me to be better. To see what life is like without the high walls and sharp borders I put around anything I can't control.

These weeks without her sassy smile in the morning or her swaying hips as she brings me a file have led to the worst insomnia of my entire life. *Two* hours on the treadmill, furiously fisting my hand, and a double of bourbon still only get me a few fitful hours of sleep. I've doubled my caffeine intake to cover it, but I can feel myself slipping. Mr. Bannister's sent more than a few worried glances my way, but since I haven't actually screwed up a case (yet), he's keeping his distance.

She still hasn't answered my calls or texts, and I'm not dense enough to believe only her study schedule is to blame. I can keep quiet, and lose the one woman who eases the constant pressure that's been plaguing me since high school, or I can come clean and risk a career that's taken years to build.

A sharp rap on my doorjamb snaps me out of my daze. Jonathan waltzes in, not bothering to wait for an invitation.

"Hey there, bestie," he says with an obnoxious grin. He's come to gloat, and I couldn't care less.

"I'm not your 'bestie', Jonathan," I reply, letting the bored irritation seep into my voice. His smile widens into a sneer and he takes a seat in one of the leather chairs of my sitting area.

"I beg to differ. We *must* be besties for you to drop that Watanabe-Moore case in my lap with a big red bow." The bastard puts his feet up on the coffee table, scuffing it with his Hugo Boss knock-offs.

"Judge Allen deliberated for less than two hours before awarding Naomi fifty percent of all marital assets, including the properties Tanner tried to hide. He also has to pay $10,000 a month in alimony, since their daughter is attending private school here, and living with Ms. Watanabe." His pleased expression nearly turns my stomach. "When this story hits the news, it's finally gonna be *my* name they say."

It stings that Jonathan gets the W after I handed everything to him on a silver platter. Still, I'm actually happy for Naomi.

Things might not have worked out between us, but I realize now that she wasn't a terrible person. Just young and maybe a little naïve, like I was. She and her daughter deserve a fresh start.

"Congratulations, Jonathan. I'm glad to hear *even you* couldn't fuck up this slam dunk of a case." His smile fades into a menacing baring of teeth and he stands.

"Hey, screw you, Henry! You may bill the most, your record may be impressive," he leans into my personal space, "but no one around here can fucking stand you." He motions to the empty desk outside my office door. "I noticed Camila wasn't out there when I came in. Did you run her off too?!"

That gets me out of my chair. I inch closer to him, blood like ice in my veins, and practically growl.

"Ms. Sanchez took a leave of absence to prepare for the bar exam." He can't hide his surprise, and I relish the opportunity to make him look like an idiot.

"She's been working and going to law school at night for years. When she passes, and I've got no doubt she'll pass, the firm would be stupid not to hire her on the spot." I lean closer to him and the pipsqueak takes a small step back. "Even without her card, she's got a better legal mind than *some* around here."

I maintain eye contact, so he knows I'm insulting him. He's not the brightest bulb in the box. To brag to me about winning with *my* work doesn't even make sense.

He puffs up his chest, trying to muster up some bravado.

"Whatever, man. Maybe I'll call her and take her someplace nice to celebrate the win. Show her not all guys at the firm are so stiff and full of themselves."

He's baiting me. I know it. Knowing it doesn't keep my hands from balling into fists, though. This moron won't get anywhere near Camila.

Just as my control starts to slip and I move further into Jonathan's space, I hear shouting down the hall.

"Get your hands off of me!" a male voice shouts. Shuffling feet and sounds of a struggle get louder as they approach my office.

"Sir, please," Avery pleads. "If you don't calm down and vacate the premises, I'll have security escort you out."

Suddenly, Tanner's body is in my doorway. His eyes are wild, and rage flows from him like water from a ruptured fire hydrant.

"You son of a bitch!" As Tanner stalks further into my office, Jonathan, the sniveling shit, sneaks out behind him.

"The board is furious. They're killing the IPO!" He kicks the coffee table, and the water glasses on top shatter to the floor. "I going to lose everything!"

I silently motion for Avery to call security while trying to guide Tanner out of my office. She scurries off in a blur of blonde waves.

"Look, Mr. Moore—" Tanner shrugs away my hand on his shoulder.

"Don't give me that 'Mr. Moore' shit. You know who I am, and I know this was *personal*."

I've nearly got him out of my office, crowding him until he has no choice but to retreat. He's not a small man—he's obviously been working out since his days on Yale crew—but I tower over him by at least four inches. That's why I made a perfect stroke, while Tanner was just a bow rower. *Maybe Camila would enjoy a few naughty crew puns...*

"I know there's bad blood between us, Tanner, but I had nothing to do with the judge's decision today. It was *you* who tried to cheat Naomi out of her fair share." Tanner just roles his eyes.

"Fair share? I built my company from nothing! Now that whore thinks she can take half of *everything*? If I'd known she was going to be this much trouble, I never would have stolen her from you all those years ago."

This guy is a piece of work. Curious heads pop out from cubicles and nearby offices, eager to catch wind of anything salacious.

"Are you seriously bringing up nonsense that happened over a decade ago?" I ask. I feel nothing like the visceral reaction I had when Naomi confronted me last week. All I feel now is relief to be done with both of them for good.

"You made this bed yourself, Tanner. Now you're gonna lie in it."

I nod to the men behind him and strong hands band around Tanner's upper arms.

"You're gonna pay for this, Henry!" Tanner yells back as security tugs him towards the elevators. "You can't hide behind these rent-a-cops forever."

I scoff at that. He *wishes* he could take me.

When security has him in the elevator and the doors close behind them, the office is at a standstill. No one is bothering to avert their eyes from the scene that unfolded.

At the back of the crowd, Mr. Bannister and Mr. Banks catch my eye, motioning for me to follow them. *Fuck*. After all that, I may have just lost my job and any opportunity to come clean about Camila. Maybe it's for the best.

"Thank you for coming, Henry," Mr. Banks says as he takes a seat next to Mr. Bannister and Mr. Smith.

As if I had a choice. I sit at the round table in the conference room reserved for partners for the second time in a week. This cannot be good.

"It has come to our attention," Mr. Smith begins, "that you are taking part in an inappropriate relationship with your paralegal, Ms. Camila Sanchez."

The floor beneath me vanishes in an instant. After days of tossing and turning, pretending I didn't know Camila was right about coming clean, and convincing myself we were being careful enough, I'm out of time. They know. *Somehow*...they know.

"What do you have to say for yourself?" Mr. Banks demands when I've stayed silent too long. I clear my throat.

"A few weeks ago," I begin hesitantly, "Ms. Sanchez and I began a casual relationship outside of the office." *Except that one time in the file room.* "It has not impacted either of our work, and the relationship does not violate any published firm policies."

Stony expressions stare back at me.

"It may not be explicitly written, Mr. Park," Mr. Banks fumes, "but you of all people know that certain rules, rules meant to preserve decorum and prevent unnecessary conflict, are implied."

"Do you plan to continue seeing Ms. Sanchez, knowing interoffice relationships are discouraged?" Mr. Bannister asks. His voice is even, his expression thoughtful.

If she'll have me. Implying that what we have is insignificant hardly helped things. Neither did suggesting we continue seeing each other in secret, considering all the women I've openly dated in the past. After the best sex of my life and an amazing weekend together, I choked at the first sign of trouble. No wonder she's not texting me back.

"I don't know," I answer honestly. Mr Banks and Mr. Smith frown.

"If you *did* choose to continue your relationship," Mr. Bannister says, "we would, of course, have to reassign Ms. Sanchez to support another attorney."

My stomach drops. I was afraid of that. But, if it means I can keep seeing her...

"I understand."

"Well, I certainly don't," Mr. Smith harrumphs. "You've put in years at this firm, Henry. Top earner six years in a row, and already in the running this year too. Why on earth would you jeopardize that for a...a *fling* with your paralegal?"

Before I can answer, Mr. Bannister cuts in.

"You're right, Sean. Henry's given us years of stellar service. And, as he mentioned, his relationship with Ms. Sanchez is not against any policies."

"Well, it damn well should be, Bill! This kind of behavior—"

"Is sometimes unavoidable, Sean," Mr. Bannister cuts in. "You know as well as I do that things can and *do* happen over long hours in close quarters. We can hardly punish Henry if he didn't break any rules, anyway."

Mr. Smith looks outraged, red-faced and shifting uncomfortably in his seat.

"A three-month suspension without pay," Mr. Banks suggests. Mr. Smith looks like he's about to explode.

"Suspension? Henry should be fired!"

"That's ridiculous," Mr. Bannister scoffs. "He's one of the finest attorneys in this firm. I agree with Richard. Three months' suspension for inappropriate conduct with a subordinate," Mr. Bannister turns his stern face to me, "and for the dust to settle with the Moore-Watanabe fiasco."

Mr. Banks nods, but Mr. Smith pushes away from the table and angrily storms out of the room. Mr. Banks sighs and follows him out.

Mr. Bannister stands, but I remain seated, still in shock. *Three months' suspension?*

"It took balls to push back about Ms. Sanchez, Henry. If you'd told us earlier, we could have addressed this more proactively."

"Yes, sir."

Mr. Bannister walks towards the door, but turns before opening it.

"Did I ever tell you about my paralegal before Cici?" I shake my head. "Annabeth. She was before your time. We travelled everywhere together. Once things changed between us, she moved to Real Estate."

He knocks on the table twice and smiles meaningfully.

"Take this time off and come back rested, Henry. You're a valuable part of this team."

Mr. Bannister opens and shuts the door behind him.

I grab a tortilla and start loading it with chicken, shredded lettuce, diced tomatoes, and cheese. I go through the motions numbly, still processing my suspension and Mr. Bannister's bombshell.

Adam and Noah wait impatiently behind me for their turn at the taco bar. I don't know how we all ended up at Mom and Dad's on a weeknight, but having family around when everything else in my life is falling apart is a blessing I won't question. *To think I ever put work over* this!

Cory is conspicuously absent. Noah's right, he's going through something, but I'm still glad I don't have to sit across the table from him when he's in the mood to lash out. Noah, on the other hand, seems to be trying to stare a hole through my face.

I ding my glass, and everyone quiets down around me.

"First, I want to say thanks, Mom and Dad, for always letting us come raid your kitchen, even though we're old enough to cook our own dinner."

"But no one throws down like Mom," Noah interjects, making Mom blush. Adam and Dad both raise their glasses in agreement.

"Second, I want to let everyone know that I'm going to be around a lot more for my baby brother's wedding planning. I won't miss anything; not a fitting, not a cake tasting. Just think of me as your wedding wingman going forward."

I take a bite of my taco, ignoring the concerned expressions that surround me. Dad is the first to speak.

"And how do you suddenly happen to have all this spare time?"

"Yeah," Adam adds. "Not to look a gift horse in the mouth, but I thought you barely had time for the wedding and now you're going to be at *everything*?"

Damn. That's what Adam thought of me? Seems like this suspension came at the perfect time. I put my taco down and look him in the eyes.

"First of all, you're my baby brother, and this is your big day. Of course I'm going to be there." I slap Adam on the back and he gives me a small smile, clearly still skeptical.

"To answer your question, Dad," I continue, "I've been suspended for three months, effective immediately." I ignore Mom's gasp. "The partners found out about Camila and I. We didn't break any rules," I rush to add when I see Dad's frown, "but between Camila, what happened with Naomi, and Tanner getting past security to threaten me—"

"What?!" Mom squeaks, and I push forward, eager to get everything out.

"They thought I should take some time off until things die down. Assuming Camila comes back after passing the bar, she will be reassigned to another department."

I take another huge bite of my taco while everyone just stares at me.

"I'm sorry to hear that, son, but you don't have to take that lying down. You can appeal. Although it's not what I would've done, if it wasn't against policy, they can't try to push you out."

I sigh and put down my taco again. It's quickly disintegrating into a pile of toppings.

"Dad, just stop. I don't need to appeal. The circumstances might not be ideal, but do you realize I haven't taken a real vacation in years? Not since before I was promoted to partner." I press on, when Dad looks ready to interrupt.

"Every time I flew somewhere, I brought my laptop. I didn't go anywhere that didn't have great Wi-Fi. For Christ's sake, I literally settled the Delancey case on the front steps of your brownstone instead of being inside to celebrate Adam's engagement. Work-life balance has been nonexistent."

Dad looks at me like I'm a petulant child rebelling against bath time.

"That's the job, son. Sure, it's more than a nine to five, but you're helping people."

I start to scoff before catching Dad's glare. I clear my throat instead.

"I don't want to keep bankers' hours, and I know the work I do is important, even if all the worst lawyer jokes are about divorce lawyers. But the pressure has been killing me, Dad. From Yale undergrad, to Yale law, to a prestigious clerkship, to the partner track, and now I'm a partner still proving myself to the *senior* partners." I tick off the list on my fingers. "There was never any break. Never any time to even think about whether all this is what I want."

"Don't be hasty, Jr.," Dad insists in a stern voice. "Don't throw away everything you've worked for just because you're a little burnt out."

My shoulders sag a bit, but I smile warmly at my father. He's my biggest role model, always pushing me to do more, think bigger. But he might have pushed too hard.

"I won't, Dad. I'm not stupid enough to throw all that education and dedication away because of one setback. All I'm saying is I'm going to use this suspension to actually take a break, to think about what I want, *who* I want, and to help my little brother get ready to walk down the aisle."

"Here, here!" Noah shouts, raising his glass. I give him a nod and drink from my own. Adam squeezes my shoulder and I catch Mom and Dad sharing a look.

"Everything's gonna be fine," I try to reassure them. "And hey, you'll get to see my handsome face more often!"

Adam laughs and throws a handful of lettuce at me.

"Full of yourself much?" he teases.

Noah puts shredded cheese down the back of my shirt while I'm dusting off the lettuce.

"Hey! What are you, twelve?"

My brothers and I devolve into a minor food fight while Mom just shakes her head. She and Dad don't have to be on board. From now on, I'm done following everyone else's plans for how my life should go. It's time to make some of my own.

CHAPTER TWENTY-SIX

Camila

I lick the powdered sugar from my fingertips and put the rest of the Pan de Mallorca away in a Tupperware container. When I close the fridge door, I catch a blurry reflection of myself and purse my lips. Finally having time to cook is a blessing and a curse if my widening hips are any indication. Unless I want to end up starring in an episode of "My 600-Lb. Life", I might need to add a walk around Orchard Beach to my new weekly routine. I might even take a dip now that the weather is getting hotter.

I rinse my plate and grab the remote, turning to NY1 News.

"...to avoid taking the 4 and 5 trains around midday today, as increased security for the president's visit to the U.N. will likely cause significant delays. In other news, it's Splitsville for fitness mogul Tanner Moore and Naomi Watanabe, an attorney who recently joined Smith, Weiss & Pratt's environmental division."

I rush to the couch and turn the volume up to hear the male anchor over the sound of my neighbor's daughter practicing the French horn. *It's summer vacation already! Give it a rest!*

"The divorce was finalized just yesterday, with BBS&P scoring another record-breaking settlement of $42 million for Ms. Watanabe. Insiders close to Ms. Watanabe reported infidelity on Moore's part. This couldn't come at a worse time for Moore, whose company, TanFit, is now reconsidering their planned IPO."

I click off the TV and smile like a fool into the silence. *Yes!* I might just be a paralegal (for now), but I got to be part of that and so many other major cases. Henry and I made a great team over the years.

Just the thought of Henry dims my smile a bit, but I push through, pulling my overstuffed binder into my lap to start today's first study block. The words are starting to blur together at this point, but I've aced the last two mock exams I took and I feel good. Plus, Henry's stopped texting, so that's...good. No more distractions.

I sigh and open my textbook to the chapter on tax law. *Ugh.* As someone who used the free software for years until Cynthia in Finance offered to look over my deductions, tax law goes way over my head. It doesn't help that the law has probably changed again since this book was written, or that the tax professor spoke in a monotone voice to rival Ben Stein. Staying awake in that class was a challenge.

Entertainment law, on the other hand, is my sweet spot. Give me copyrights, licensing agreements, and contracts with ten-page riders and I'm golden. I'm already in New York, the second best place behind LA to make a career in entertainment law.

A tiny, wild thought tinkles like a wind chime in the back of my head. *Doesn't Henry's brother, Noah, work in entertainment?* I shake my head, trying to dispel the idea, but it quickly takes root and spreads.

It's smart to have a job lined up for after I pass the bar. I don't think I can go back to working for Henry... I get up and start pacing. *I doubt Noah would mind if I stopped by. It's just a chat, maybe over coffee. What's the worst that could happen?*

I wrack my brain, trying to come up with a valid excuse not to contact Noah, but come up blank. Sure, it might be a little awkward to work for my ex's brother. But Henry isn't even really an ex! And he's the epitome of professional. He would never hold it against me for pursuing a legitimate career opportunity in an industry where *who* you know outweighs *what* you know ten to one.

With the idea still forming in my head, I slam my textbook closed and jog back to my room. I yank on a navy pants suit and a cream blouse with ruffles around the collar from my closet. It's already been a couple months since Noah met; I need to hurry before he forgets my face.

This was not a good idea. Sitting in a reception area that looks more like an Apple store than a talent management firm, all the reasons I shouldn't have come start rushing through my head.

It could be awkward working for Noah after how personal things got with Henry. Henry might've already told Noah things got personal and now he expects the same thing. No, I don't think Noah's a creep. *Henry might've already told Noah things ended badly, so he sends me packing to back up his brother. Noah might not even be here, since I showed up without an appointment like a psychopath.*

I'm spiraling and my palms are sweating. I nervously tuck a curl behind my ear and will that tiny line of perspiration on my upper lip to evaporate before anyone sees. I can't risk wiping and messing up my makeup.

"Ms. Sanchez?" the receptionist calls. She can't be more than twenty-five and looks like she could be in movies herself. I rise from the kidney bean-shaped couch and come to the desk.

"Hello," I whisper. She hands me a visitor's badge and points toward a bank of elevators.

"Take the middle elevator to the 20th floor. The receptionist there will walk you back." I smile mutedly and walk to the elevator, clutching my folio for dear life. It's too late to turn back now. He already knows I'm here.

Once I'm off the elevator, I follow another actress-slash-receptionist down the hall to Noah's office. *God, my heels are making a lot of noise on the floor. Why am I freaking out right now? I'm just an acquaintance stopping by. It's not even a job interview. Not yet, anyway. Nothing to be—*

"Camila! Hi!" Noah stands from behind his desk, a warm smile on his face. I feel immediately at ease. He takes my hand in both of his and leads me to sit down on one of the magenta armchairs in front of his desk, surprising me by taking the other one.

"So," he says, leaning back in his chair. "What brings you here for a surprise visit?" I smile sheepishly.

"Sorry for the unannounced drop-in." Noah waves his hand like my explanation is unnecessary, like even thinking I needed an explanation is ridiculous.

"No worries at all. I've always got a few minutes for my bro's right-hand woman. What's up?"

I steel my nerves, trying not to imagine that everyone is staring at us through the glass walls of Noah's office.

"Well, as you know, I've worked for Henry for several years. Do you also know I've been going to law school?" Noah nods.

"Henry mentioned it." Great. That's one less thing to explain.

"Right. So, I just graduated a couple weeks ago, and when I pass the bar, I was thinking about specializing in entertainment law." He raises a quizzical eyebrow.

"Six years doing divorce law under my brother and now you want to get into entertainment?" I shuffle my feet nervously before catching myself.

"I can understand how it seems unusual. I never planned on going into divorce law, but your brother is the best, and I wanted to work for the best."

Brotherly pride is apparent on his face. I rush to take out my resume, which he accepts without hesitation.

"I can give you a copy of my transcript too, if you need it. I excelled in contract law, intellectual property law, and employment law. I even took a seminar on licensing led by the Harry Fox Agency."

Noah peruses my resume, obviously impressed.

"And, I assume, you can provide a stellar recommendation from Henry?" My nervous smile droops a little.

"Well," I clear my throat, "Henry is aware I'm interested in entertainment law, and I'm currently on a leave of absence from BBS&P to study for the bar, but...I haven't yet advertised my intention to leave the firm."

Noah steeples his hands and a wrinkle appears on his brow.

"Your tenure with Henry is already a gold star on your resume—I know how much of a rigid pain in the ass he can be—but don't you want to let him know you're looking elsewhere? Keeping something like that a secret from my brother puts me in a bit of a tight spot."

I sigh and reach for my resume, but he pulls it away.

"Whoa, whoa! Wait a minute. I'm not saying no. We definitely could use another attorney on staff, but why can't you just give Henry a heads up so he's not caught off guard?" I grip my folio even tighter and try to swallow as quietly as possible.

"Are you aware that Henry and I..." I trail off, hoping he can fill in the rest.

"That you're in a relationship? Yes. But my brother would be happy for his girlfriend to pursue such a great opportunity, even if it's not at BBS&P." My heart lurches at the word "girlfriend" and I fiddle with the frilly cuff of my shirt. I can't meet his eyes.

"'Girlfriend' would be a bit strong for what we were. And, regardless, that is over now. That's kind of why I'm looking to make my leave of absence more permanent." I slump against my chair. "I'm sorry. I knew this was probably a long shot and potentially inappropriate, but—"

Noah reaches his hand out to stop my babbling, a serious expression on his face.

"I'm sorry, Camila. I didn't know." He lifts the corner of his mouth, trying to lighten the mood. It's not quite a smile.

"Even so, I'm sure he'd give you the recommendation if you talked with him. My word will go a long way, but HR and the other partners will still want a recommendation on file, especially if it comes from a partner at BBS&P."

"Yeah, maybe so," I mutter, already knowing I won't talk to Henry. Not any time soon, anyway. It's still too raw, and I'm too...embarrassed.

Out of nowhere, Noah slaps his knee and stands up. He gestures towards the door.

"Come on. I'll walk you down to the Director of HR, Tammy Klein. It won't hurt to leave your info on file. That way, when your recommendation comes in, it'll be a piece of cake to make an offer."

I smile weakly and stand to follow him.

"Sure. That sounds great. Thank you, again, for even meeting with me today."

He shoos my apology away and continues to lead us towards an office at the end of the hall.

"It's nothing. Seriously. But talk to Henry. Even if you two don't work it out, he's a standup guy. He'll make sure you're taken care of."

Noah gives me a wink and the fist gripping my heart tightens even further. They are almost identical and yet nothing alike. Noah is relaxed, with a fun, playful energy. Henry's energy is more like a school principal or a police captain. Unless we were together, he hardly smiled, let alone winked.

Thinking about Henry as "playful" is almost laughable...until I remember our last weekend together. He let me see so many sides to him I never knew existed. But when it came time to go public, suddenly Sub Zero was back.

I blink away the sudden moisture in my eyes and follow Noah to Tammy's office. Before I head in, I take a deep breath and square my shoulders. *On to bigger and better things, Camila.*

CHAPTER TWENTY-SEVEN

Henry

Adam stands in front of the full-length mirrors, admiring himself in the navy blue tux. The break has too many folds, and there are a few extra inches in the midsection that will need to be taken in. Necessary alterations aside, he looks great. The color is flattering, and any suit paired with the limited edition Santoni shoes he doesn't know I'm gifting him is bound to look good. To me though, a notch lapel says "business meeting" not "one of the most important days of my life". At my wedding, I'll probably go for something more formal.

I swirl the complimentary Jameson around in my glass and let the clink of the ice cubes soothe me. I must be drunk. There's no other reason why NYC's top divorce attorney would suddenly fantasize about his own wedding. I know the numbers. I know the heartbreak. On paper, marriage just doesn't work. But if you put that paper down and look at the amazing woman standing in front of you...it's understandable why so many people take the leap.

I shake my head and put my tumbler down on the mirrored coffee table. I *must* be drunk. Adam turns again to look over his shoulder at the back of his suit.

"What do we think?" he asks everyone. The private fitting room at Robbie & Co.'s is impressive. Besides free drinks, there's a flatscreen showing the Mets stomping the Red Sox, and Cory and Noah are enjoying a lively game of billiards.

"Scratch!" Cory shouts triumphantly when Noah knocks the white ball into the pocket. Adam rolls his eyes and turns back to the mirror. I glare at them both the way only the eldest brother can.

"C'mon, guys," I chastise. "We're here to help our baby brother get married, not start a blood feud over what should be a friendly game of pool."

Noah and Cory look sufficiently scolded and join me on the couch. Cory gestures limply at Adam.

"That one looks great on you," Cory says blandly. He's said that about every suit Adam has tried on today.

"I like the color, but..." Noah trails off, considering.

"But it doesn't seem formal enough?" I offer. Noah slaps his knee.

"That's it! I couldn't figure out what was bothering me about it. It says 'I do taxes', not 'I do'."

Adam ignores the juvenile gagging sound coming from Cory and looks himself over again. Doubt clouds his expression.

"Why don't you try something with a shawl lapel?" I suggest, taking another swig of my whiskey even though the ice has watered it down. Adam's face brightens.

"I can do that. Be right back." Adam takes off to the fitting room and Cory doesn't hide his smirk.

"Our baby brother is the definition of 'whipped'. I can't believe he's the first to settle down. It's like all our training meant nothing to him." Noah reaches over and smacks the back of Cory's head.

"Cut it out, bro," Noah warns. "Adam is happy with Maya. He clearly loves her. Don't be a dick and rain on his parade."

Cory falls against the back of the couch, resigned to attend the tux fitting but hell bent on complaining every step of the way.

Noah risks a glance in my direction from across the pool table, then uses lightning fast reflexes to pretend he wasn't looking. He's been staring at me off and on since I announced my suspension. When Cory jumps up to go to the men's room, I turn to find Noah, yet again, staring at me.

"What's with all the weird looks?" I ask, foregoing small talk to get straight to the meat of the issue. A rueful smile tugs at Noah's lips.

"I just...don't know where we stand," he admits hesitantly. "I wouldn't have even come today, since I thought it would be awkward, but, you know, it's mandatory."

"Of course it is. You don't want to end up looking like a hobo in an off-the-rack suit if Adam decides to go bespoke."

Noah chuckles lightly, but his smile doesn't reach his eyes. We're both silent for a while.

"I really am sorry about what happened," Noah mutters before taking a sip of his Maker's Mark.

"I know you are," I sigh. "We're good. I just...It just felt like, when Adam and Cory both knew about Naomi, all of you had been laughing at me behind my back." Noah rears back, offended.

"That's not how it was at all! You might not remember, but you were a real pain in the ass for *months* after it happened. I finally broke down and told the others so they'd stop worrying about you."

Wow. I never realized my brothers care enough to worry about me.

"And the stuff about Camila?" I ask, eyebrow raised. Noah's excuse for telling them about Naomi seems plausible enough, but why the hell would he need to give anyone details about what I did with Camila? His expression turns chagrined.

"That was just one too many Maker's Marks. As soon as it came out, I knew I'd made a mistake." I grunt and drain the rest of my glass.

"I'm not saying it's cool, but thanks for telling me what happened. Camila is really special to me." Noah waggles his eyebrows suggestively.

"Oooh! She is, is she?" I brace myself for some brotherly ball busting. "So when do Mom & Dad and the other brothers get to meet her? Is she coming to the wedding?"

I wish I knew. I shrug and stand to take Cory's place at the pool table.

"Did Mom tell you Damon changed his flight? He'll be here a full two weeks before the big day." I silently pray Noah lets me get away with changing the subject yet again. The look on his face says "no such luck".

"You know she reached out to me about a week ago," Noah says. He casually gets up for another drink at the bar, like he didn't just drop a nuke on my brain.

"She who?" I ask, hoping he's talking about someone else. He turns and looks at me like I'm a moron. OK. So we're clearly talking about Mila.

"Well, what did she want?" I ask, trying to control the pleading tone of my voice. Noah's smile turns a little wicked. Although he accused Cory of enjoying holding things over people's heads, that was definitely the pot calling the kettle black.

"It was about work, actually. She asked if there were any entry-level positions at my firm, something a new lawyer could use to cut their teeth." Noah tries to cover his laughter at my stunned face with a cough. He fails miserably.

"She reached out for a *job*?!" The gravity of his words hits me like a bucket of ice water. *What is she doing looking for jobs? She's coming back once she passes the bar, isn't she?* My palms start to sweat.

"Hey bro, chill," Noah says in a soothing tone. He pats me awkwardly on the shoulder. "It was just a meeting. Nothing is set in stone. I took her resume and set up a meeting for her with

HR. That's it." Hearing Camila's thinking of leaving the firm, of leaving *me*...

"Are you going to hire her?" I croak. I'm having a hard time catching my breath. Noah's eyes dart away uncomfortably.

"I mean," he starts, avoiding eye contact, "what firm wouldn't want someone with 5+ years of experience supporting a partner at BBS&P, even a paralegal? And she'll have her J.D. from Syracuse soon?"

He waves his hand like the answer is obvious and I gulp because it is. Painfully. Noah leans over for another stiff pat on my shoulder.

"Don't start panicking yet, bro. I told her nothing could move forward without a recommendation from you. Honestly, I thought she might have talked to you about it already, but obviously not."

"Well...I guess that's something. Now she'll have to talk to me." Noah sees a bad idea brewing and thankfully intervenes.

"And you'll do the right thing like you always do, and you won't hold her career hostage just because things didn't work out. Right?" The doubt in his voice is enough to squash the idiotic notion before it can take root. I won't deny her the recommendation—her work is stellar, and she's had to deal with my bullshit on top of all of that—but if she thinks we're not talking about us, she's crazy.

While my whole world is imploding around me, Adam comes out from the dressing room with Cory hot on his heels. Adam's wearing a black velvet tux with a satin shawl lapel. There's subtle paisley on the velvet, which I thought would be too trendy when I saw it on the mannequin, but it actually works. He looks incredible. He knows it too, judging by the way he's smiling at his reflection in the mirrors.

"That's the one," Noah and I both say, then laugh. We never did much of the twin speak, even as kids, but we're clearly on the same page about that beautiful suit. Even Cory looks impressed, though he opts not to say anything. Adam turns to see the suit from another angle.

"I think you're both right. This suit is the one," Adam says. I stand with my glass raised, swaying a bit from the two previous glasses.

"Here's to Adam. He's the perfect brother, marrying the perfect girl, in the perfect suit." Cory laughs and yanks me back down to sit, but drinks anyway.

"Sit down, man. You always get so emotional when you drink."

Noah and Adam are both smiling too and it feels good between all of us for the first time in a while. Nothing, not a new relationship, not moving to Westchester, not even a huge fight, can break the bonds of brotherhood. Once Damon is back for the wedding, things will be perfect.

Well, almost perfect. My heart squeezes when I remember that the person I want to be my date for the wedding, the one person I might actually consider taking the plunge with, as scary as that feels, is planning to leave for good. If she needs a grand gesture to know how I feel about her, then a grand gesture is what she's fucking going to get.

CHAPTER TWENTY-EIGHT

Camila

"Bye, guys! Next time, I'll bring my Critical Pass flash-cards. They're a total game changer for some of those tricky multiple-choice questions."

Kyle, a lanky twenty-something with dirty blonde hair, oversized glasses, and a prominent nose, bows his thanks and Amina, a short Indian woman in full makeup, blows a kiss before they disappear down the stairs to the F train. They're both five years younger than I am and look like they walked straight out of an Old Navy ad. Also, they have their shit down.

Joining the in-person study group was long overdue. With Kyle and Amina's help, I finally feel like I'm moving past rote memorization to full comprehension. As a proud Bronxite, it stings that they're both from Queens, but they're still good people. I'm going to make this test my bitch!

As soon as I reach the escalators at Penn Station, I pop my headphones in and crank the volume up to eleven. Initially, I spent every waking moment studying, even downloading exam prep podcasts to listen to on the subway. But with the test coming up next week and my anxiety at an all-time high, I've started forcing myself to take breaks. My newest rule? Music only music during my commute.

Celia Cruz sings a song of yearning as I push past the rush hour traffic and feel a twinge of guilt that I'm not at work. Yes, it's common to take time off for exam prep, especially at a law firm. Yes, since I left, I've been getting the best sleep of my life and exploring parts of the city I've been neglecting. But I know I didn't leave in the most professional way.

I also know I owe Henry more than the cold shoulder after years of working together. Just because things didn't work out between us, it doesn't mean we can't be civil. I'll need to talk to him about that recommendation, anyway. Maybe I'll stop by reception tomorrow and see if I can catch him at lunch.

As I turn onto my street, familiar horn-rimmed glasses catch my eye. Or, I can talk to him *now*, since Henry's currently leaning against the railing in front of my building. *What the hell?*

I try to slow down, maybe duck between the buildings to take the back entrance, but he sees me anyway. He straightens and nervously wipes one hand on his pants, holding a bouquet of purple flowers in the other. In jeans and a blazer, he looks more like one of my professors than a legal shark. *Fuck me if that doesn't make him look even hotter.*

I come to a stop two feet in front of him, leaving enough space so I won't just jump into his arms on instinct. *I've missed him!* He pushes his glasses further up his nose and I can see his Adam's apple bob as he swallows.

"What are you doing here, Henry?" I hate how accusatory that sounded, but I still feel a bit raw.

"I—" He clears his throat. "I wanted to see you. I brought you these." He awkwardly pushes the flowers in my direction and I simply stare at them.

"The florist said hyacinth is for forgiveness," he adds, still holding the flowers out to me. After another moment of hesitation, I take the bouquet. I'm a little pissed at how beautiful it is, and that he thought to ask the florist for a recommendation. Sub Zero was never this thoughtful, which means I'm talking to Henry. But which one?

"Thank you. This is really...sweet." One corner of his mouth lifts in a small smile and the silence stretches between us. As usual, I'm the first to break it.

"Don't get me wrong, the flowers are beautiful, but I still don't know why you're here. It's 4:30pm on a Thursday. Shouldn't you be at work?"

He shifts uncomfortably before meeting my eyes.

"I've been suspended. For three months." I gasp and nearly drop the flowers and all my bags.

"What?! What happened?" Henry shrugs like the biggest twist since the ending of "Fight Club" is nothing to him.

"The senior partners weren't too happy with how things went down with Naomi. Asking to be taken off such a high-profile case is extremely unusual, even with inappropriate behavior on the client's part." He sighs.

"They would've let it go...but then...someone reported us. If not for Bannister, I'd be out of a job."

I feel a pain in my palm and realize I have the strap of my satchel in a death grip.

"That bitch."

"What?" Henry says, clearly surprised by my reaction.

"It was Vanessa." His eyes widen.

"Vanessa? How would she have known?"

I sigh and lean against the railing next to him.

"That day I left? The day of the kiss?" Henry drops his eyes, obviously reliving that terrible memory.

"She was standing right outside the door. I'm not sure how much she heard, but when I saw her, she accused me of sleeping with you to get my position. Apparently, she's been pissed at me this whole time."

Henry's jaw is like granite, his eyes filled with lethal intent.

"She said that to you?"

I shrug.

"As you know, I can handle the assholes at work. I thought it was just some catty bullshit. But you're saying she went to the partners?"

"Either she did, or she told Jonathan and he did," Henry growls.

All the more reason to get out of dodge.

"They really almost fired you? For something that isn't technically against the rules?"

"Actually, it was like you said."

I look at him, confused.

"They weren't happy, but I got in more trouble because I didn't tell them beforehand. Once someone filed a report, there weren't a lot of options."

I don't say "I told you so", but I think it.

"You can go ahead and say it," he says with a smirk. "I fucked up. I knew it as soon as you walked out the door, but I thought we'd have a chance to talk it out."

"Henry. I..." I raise and drop my hand, unsure what to say, where to start.

Henry chuckles.

"It's honestly no big deal." I furrow my brow. "I mean, it *is* a big deal, but it feels like it was meant to be. Seven years is way too long to go with practically no down time. No vacation, staying late every night, and working through every weekend? It was a recipe for disaster. If it hadn't been this, it would have been something else."

I'm struggling to come to terms with the firm's top earner spouting the virtues of stopping to smell the roses. It's unheard of.

"Well...I can't say I'm not surprised. I'm *beyond* surprised. But if you're able to embrace this whole situation and finally take some much needed time off, then I'm happy for you. You definitely earned it."

Henry gives me a genuine smile and I'm thankful to be already leaning against the railing.

"I'm also here to warn you," he says. Something shifts in his eyes. He's gone from unsure to determined, even cocky.

"Warn me?" I reply, raising an eyebrow. He just smirks in response.

"Yes. I'm here to warn you I'm not giving up on us. You can storm out of the office over a mistake." He raises an arm when I open my mouth to interrupt. "A mistake I regretted immediately, even more than not pushing Naomi when she put her hand on my knee."

His face is obviously contrite, and my heart squeezes.

"You can ignore my calls and texts. You can bury yourself in studying—which I totally get, by the way. But soon, when you're done with the bar and can add *Esquire* to your name, we're going to talk. We're going to talk and you're going to hear me out and stop being so stubborn."

"I'm not being stubborn," I argue, ignoring the juvenile pout in my voice. He gives me an adoring smile in return.

"You *are* stubborn, but it's OK. I'm not perfect either." He looks into my eyes, emotion swirling right at the surface. There's lust there, and determination to get his way; it's part of what makes him a formidable lawyer. There's also something else. Something too big for me to process on five hours of sleep with a week still left on my study plan. He must sense my inner turmoil.

"I'm not here to get into everything right now; there'll be time for that later. You're probably beside yourself with nerves over the test next week." I can't help but nod.

"That's totally normal. Just stick with your schedule, make sure that schedule includes sleep, and the day before the exam, don't study at all. Give your brain a break. Once you pass, and you're *going* to pass," he says with a certainty that makes me grin, "we're going to talk and we're going to get past this."

He lifts the hand not holding a tote full of binders and kisses my knuckles. His velvet soft lips have me wishing he'd come upstairs, study plan be damned. Instead, he winks and heads to the waiting car parked in front of my building. I give Murray a small wave; his only response is a knowing smile.

CHAPTER TWENTY-NINE

Camila

"Alright, everyone! Pencils and pens down!" the proctor announces. A collective sigh fills the room, along with a few distraught wails. After two grueling days—essays on day one and multiple-choice questions on day two—I'm officially done with the bar. I know I passed. I can *feel* it.

I bring my Scantron sheet to the front of the auditorium and then head back to gather my belongings. I opted to take the exam at the Judicial Institute at Pace rather than in the city because I thought the commute would be less stressful and the room a little less crowded. The commute was still a pain—I took a car before the sun was up rather than risk public transit—but the campus is beautiful, and I had time for a light breakfast at a nearby cafe.

All packed up, I make my way to the front entrance, sur-rounded by people that look as tired as I feel. Some form a group and wander off in search of food. A few meet friends or family members with pride in their eyes, pulling them into embraces. Rory and Gabe offered to come, but I figured I would be too beat to celebrate. Now, I really wish I had a hug and a bed to fall into; preferably a bed that doesn't cost $70 in cab fare to get to.

I take out my phone to call a car, but see a text message waiting for me instead.

Henry

Henry: Hey. Look up. ;-)

I scan the area until I see Henry leaning against his car in visitor parking. Murray's nowhere to be found; Henry must have driven himself. He's wearing a blue button down that's rolled up over his forearms, jeans that hug his muscular legs, and a smile that says he's up to no good. When he sees me spot him, he motions for me to join him at the car. I walk over, but still keep my distance.

"You certainly weren't joking about showing up to talk as soon as I finished the exam. I kinda hoped I'd have a chance to sleep first, though."

He laughs and takes my bag, putting his arm around my shoulders and guiding me to the passenger side of his car. The warmth of his touch sears right through my flimsy cotton t-shirt. Ever the gentleman, he opens my door, closing it once I'm seated. I'm hit with the smell of something rich and savory, and my stomach growls like a wild animal in response. Then Henry gets in, and I'm enveloped by the scent of fresh linen and leather binding like what they use for those giant law journals. *Great.* Now I'm hungry for food *and* sex.

"Don't worry. The first thing I'm doing is taking you home to get some rest. If you're anything like I was, you're liable to sleep for twenty-four hours straight. You can fall asleep on the drive if you want, but I figured you'd be hungry. I remember being too nervous to eat much of anything when I took the test."

He places a to-go container in my lap and I waste no time tearing into it. It's filled with a chicken shawarma wrap, falafel, and tabbouleh—my frequent lunch order at BBS&P. I barely get my seatbelt buckled before taking a bite.

"Mmthank myou," I say around a mouthful of food. He laughs again and puts the car in gear.

Once we're on the highway, he breaks the comfortable silence. Well, silent except for the sound of me demolishing my Middle Eastern feast.

"So, how do you think you did?" he asks without looking at me, eyes locked on the road.

"I don't want to jinx anything," I hedge. There's no need to tempt fate just because I have a good feeling. But there is something to be said for manifesting the reality you want...

"Actually, screw that. I aced it," I amend, and take another big bite of my wrap. I can see amusement in the curve of Henry's mouth.

"As if there was any doubt. Between working at BBS&P, law school, and studying almost 24/7 for the past few months, you probably could've passed that test in your sleep. Still, I'll keep my fingers and toes crossed just in case."

I nod and go back to my meal. I'm so starving I'm not even embarrassed by how quickly I'm stuffing my face. It's his fault for getting me such a delicious meal.

He turns on the radio and we're serenaded by Top 40 hits...for all of ten minutes. Before I know what's happening, we've pulled into the driveway of an impressive Tudor-style house. There's a cobblestone path leading up to the front door, manicured bushes in front of the first-story windows, and tall trees surrounding us.

Henry takes my things from the backseat and jumps out of the car. When I don't immediately follow, he knocks on the passenger side window.

"Hey. Are you coming out?" He smirks at my bewildered expression and opens my door.

"Where are we?" I ask. If he's kidnapping me, at least he's not keeping me in a dungeon. *Wait. Is there a dungeon?*

"Home, like I said." He takes off up the sidewalk before I can ask any more questions and I follow him, still amazed. This house has to be at least 4,000 square feet!

He opens the heavy front door with a keypad and we enter a huge foyer complete with a chandelier because, *of course* he has a fucking chandelier. I'm suddenly very embarrassed about my little two-bedroom apartment. He makes a sweeping gesture toward exposed beams, arched doorways, and grand fireplaces. Ornate rugs sit atop pristine hardwood and rich leather couches make the space more inviting. This house could be in Architectural Digest.

"So, this is my place. I'll save the tour for after your nap."

I'm still speechless. He takes my hand and guides me up a staircase, past several open doors—a bathroom, what looks like his study, a guest room—and opens the door to what must be the master suite. I stare agog at the king size bed in the middle.

"Henry...your place. It's seriously impressive." *Is it weird that this house is making me wet?* He smiles with pride and puts my things on a chaise lounge chair by the window.

"Thanks. I had a decorator come in, so I can hardly take the credit. My brothers tease me, saying it's nothing like the city, but that's what I love about it." He strides to a walk-in closet I didn't even see when I came in and comes out with an oversized t-shirt and a pair of athletic shorts.

"These should fit you, but let me know if they don't and I'll find something else. The bathroom's in there." He points to the right before heading back into the closet.

The bathroom is just as outrageous as the rest of the house. First off, it's bigger than my college dorm. There's a jacuzzi tub with jets. The rain head shower has marble tiles on three sides. Hell, even the double vanity is marble. Weird or not, this house is definitely making my lady parts tingle.

I should maybe shower—I definitely sweat through my shirt during the exam—but I'm just too exhausted. Henry's shirt stretches tightly across my sizable breasts, but it'll be fine for a nap. The shorts, however, are another story. They barely make it halfway up my thighs. I leave them in a heap with my other clothes by the toilet (*which has a fuckin' bidet!*) and look at myself in the mirror. My curves are curvin' right now!

I'm sure Henry won't mind me sleeping bottomless. I peek through the door at the bed and sigh. It sucks I'm too tired to jump his bones right now. Between the ride, the food, and the resort-level accommodations, he's definitely earned it.

I come back into the room to find Henry getting into the bed in just his boxers.

"Uh, what are you doing?" Henry pats the spot on the bed next to him.

"What does it look like? I'm taking a nap."

"I thought *I* was taking a nap. You know. *Alone.*" He pats the spot again.

"Nope," he says, popping the P. "We're taking a nap *together* because I haven't had a good night's sleep since you left." I wobble on my knees before righting myself against the mattress. *That's major.*

He pats the bed again and I finally get in. When he rolls over and wraps his arms around me, it feels like the most natural thing in the world. Like we've always been big spoon and little spoon.

I instinctively arch my back into the hardness behind me, and he squeezes a boob in retaliation.

"Hey! No hanky panky! Sleep first."

I giggle through a pout, snuggle deeper against his chest, and immediately fall asleep.

CHAPTER THIRTY

Camila

It's pitch black in here. I literally cannot see my hand in front of my face. I feel around for Henry...No Henry. OK, so, how the hell do I even find the light switch?

I fumble around in the sheets again and my hand brushes against something small and plastic. A remote. It feels like there are only two buttons, so it can't be for the TV. I press one and nothing happens. When I press the second one, thick curtains reveal the late afternoon sun as it cascades off the pool. The *pool*! That's it. I hope Henry and I can work things out because I'm moving in.

I take care of my bathroom needs and decide to look for Henry. To be honest, I just want to snoop through his house.

The hallway bathroom is just as luxurious as the master, minus the jacuzzi, and the study is something out of Bond film.

Before I can peek into the guest room, I hear music coming from downstairs and follow it on tip toes.

Around the corner from a chef's kitchen, and past the game room, I find the source of the music: a gym. Not just any gym. A *fully equipped* gym with machines I don't even recognize. A professional athlete would kill for this gym. Henry's currently doing pull-ups...shirtless...glistening. *Dios mío!*

He catches my reflection in the mirror and gives me a smile so hot, I definitely need a shower now. I might need a moment alone with those jets in his jacuzzi tub.

He lets himself slowly drop, grinning when my eyes trace the movement. Like a predator, he prowls up to me and kisses me hard on the lips. *Thank God I brushed my teeth!*

"Hey, sleepyhead. I was starting to wonder whether I should call a doctor." I roll my eyes.

"What time is it?"

"Just after five. You slept almost twenty-four hours."

"It *feels* like it. I'm rested for the first time in like a year." He weaves my fingers between his and leads us back toward the stairs.

"Good."

His voice is deeper than I've ever heard it, and with each step, his eyes burn into mine. I almost trip over the rug in the hallway.

"How long did *you* sleep?" I ask, struggling to maintain my self-control as he studies me so intensely. Yesterday, he said he couldn't sleep without me, but that had to be an exaggeration. That kind of thing only happens in love songs.

Back in the bedroom, he drops his sweat towel into the hamper by the dresser.

"Twelve hours." My eyes widen and he nods. "I know. That's unheard of for me."

I walk towards the bathroom and lean against the doorjamb. I'll cave without some space between us. Especially if he's going to sit on the bed, legs spread wide, and stare at me like a hungry wolf. Clearly, I'm not the only one feeling the heat.

"You said you wanted to talk when I finished the bar, so talk." I cross my arms when he stays silent, and he sighs.

"Yes, you're right. First, I want to say I'm sorry for kissing Naomi. Yes, she started it, but I should've ended it right away and I didn't." I raise my hands to stop him.

"As much as it pisses me off that you kissed her, that's not why I left. Well, that's not the main reason I left. You and I are just hanging out, right? We don't belong to each other."

Henry stands, and I can tell he's agitated by the bunch in his shoulders.

"All these years later, and I'm still making the same mistakes," he mutters to himself. He turns and looks me square in the eyes.

"If not for that bullshit with Naomi, I would've asked you that day. I thought it was clear after our night together; I want to be with you."

For the hundredth time in the last few weeks, one thought runs through my head: *Fuck Naomi.* I blow out a frustrated breath.

"If that's true, why the hell did you want to keep us a secret? I remember what you said. You said you wanted to wait to tell them until it was 'worth it'." I make air quotes. "I felt like such a bonehead because I thought we already *were* worth it." His face is pained.

"I'm so sorry, Camila. I panicked. I was trying to save my job, and I lost everything anyway."

Unshed tears blur my eyes, and I wipe them away. Henry starts pacing.

"Weeks into my suspension, I haven't missed BBS&P once, but I've missed you every day." He takes my hands in his.

"I went back to Artuso Pastry Shop and bought about five black-and-white cookies. I got way too drunk when I went back to The Commodore, hoping I might run into you. I even started watching one of those K-dramas on Netflix because I know you love them.

"And I couldn't fucking sleep. I've never really been a good sleeper. Ever since high school, I just couldn't wind down. I had a tested system to get as much sleep as possible that worked for years. But then when we started hanging out, I noticed I didn't need any of that. Even the first night we kissed, I didn't even remember falling asleep." I give him a rueful smile and pat his hand.

"I think that might've been the alcohol," I interrupt, but he shakes his head.

"I thought so too, but then it happened again, the night after the file room. And after that first night in your apartment. And,

of course, you know about the last time in your apartment."
I turn to hide my blush.

"Something about you just..." He shrugs. "I don't know. It relaxes me. The world doesn't seem so heavy, like maybe I don't need all my rules and systems to make sense of everything."

I lower my eyes, at a loss for words. He tilts my chin up so we're face to face.

"Then, when you left, all that stopped. The tossing and turning was back, and even my system didn't work. I swam laps, I worked out until I couldn't stand, and I jerked off near constantly, but I could never sleep more than two hours at a time. It's you. The difference is you."

He kisses me with agonizing sweetness, and the tears spill down my face.

"After years at my side, I've finally found you. Please tell me I haven't lost you."

I kiss him again and press my forehead to his. *That's one hell of a closing argument.*

"You haven't lost me. I'm right here."

He nuzzles his nose against the tender spot behind my ear, and I shiver, pressing my breasts into his chest. We stumble backwards, kissing and groping our way into the bathroom.

I step back to ease my shirt over my head and stand before him, wearing nothing but my most seductive smile. His eyes blaze as he looks at me, chest rising with each labored breath.

"You weren't wearing any panties this whole time?"

I blink innocently, and his eyes burn even hotter before he shucks down his shorts and boxer briefs in one swoop. He pulls me in for another kiss, his tongue pushing into my mouth. I don't even care that he's sweaty. After a solid thirty seconds of making out, he pulls away and his voice is breathless against my face.

"Before things get out of hand," he pants, "would you be my date for my brother's wedding?" He lifts my hand and places gentle kisses on my fingers. "It's in two weeks."

My jaw goes slack.

"Won't your whole family be there? Like your parents and all your brothers?" He looks at me like I'm crazy, but keeps kissing my hands.

"Uh, yeah. It's my brother's wedding."

"And you want *me* there?" He kisses me again and lets go of my hands to squeeze my ass.

"Yes, Camila, I want you there. It doesn't get more public than that."

Holy shit. Henry watches me attentively as I worry my lip in thought. *Fuck it.* I love him. I kiss his mouth softly until the wrinkle on his forehead disappears.

"Yeah," I answer. "Yes, I'll be your date."

He beams and reaches behind me to turn the shower on. I trail my fingers down the ridges of abs Michelangelo could have sculpted, and a condom materializes from the drawer beside the sink. Thank God we're done talking!

He's crowding me, nudging me backwards until my skin collides with cold tiles. He leans in and bites my shoulder, and the slight pain paired with the feel of the warm water flowing down my skin is intoxicating. I'm seconds from melting into a puddle of horny girl goo, but something's been bothering me. I put my hand on his chest.

"Henry, wait. Real quick: How did you know where I'd be for the test?" He nips my neck again and looks chagrinned.

"I didn't. I took a shot you'd choose the location closest to your place." He shrugs. "If you weren't here, I was going to stand outside your door again and beg for forgiveness."

I cover my mouth, but I can't stop the giggle from escaping. He laughs too, then takes my wrists in his hands. He pulls a loofah from behind me and adds body wash, lathering it until suds drip onto the floor. The smell of verbena surrounds us.

Sufficiently soapy, he drags the loofah down my body, starting at my neck and shoulders. He pays special attention to each nipple and the sensitive space between my breasts. He gently massages both hips and the swell of my lower belly. His hand ventures lower still, to where my thighs meet, tenderly rubbing the soap into my mons, between my folds.

I gasp when the loofah is replaced by slick fingers probing my opening as his thumb presses against my clit.

"Oh, yessss," I sigh, letting my head fall back against the tiles.

He swallows my moans with another scorching kiss and starts a rhythm in and out of my soaking channel. My legs begin to quiver involuntarily, and he curls his fingers against my G-spot while caressing my bud until I'm on the edge of insanity.

"I can feel you pulsing around my fingers," he says, his voice hoarse.

"I'm close," I whimper, and he lets out a wicked laugh before ducking down to suck a nipple into his mouth. His tongue laps the tight peak like a decadent treat, and I'm nearly overcome with sensation.

"Cum for me now," he growls.

Clinging to him, I obey, shattering against his hand and biting my lip to contain my scream. He reaches up and pulls my lip from between my teeth.

"Uh uh. Not tonight. What's the point of having this big house if I can't make you scream in every room? Don't worry; my nearest neighbors are half a mile away." I laugh and fall back against the tile.

"Noted."

I grab the condom from by the sink before picking up the forgotten loofah. With my hands on his shoulders, I gently steer Henry towards a bench in the corner of the shower.

"My turn."

I push him down to sitting and wedge my hips between his legs. He instinctively grabs onto them, kissing and biting any flesh he can reach. I lean over his body, pressing my mound against his chest so I can wash his back. He grabs my ass to keep me from toppling forward, a middle finger slipping into my passage from behind. I gasp, but I don't stop lathering.

Once his back is clean enough to eat off of, I wash my way down his impressive chest to focus my efforts on his aching cock. It's pointing at me like it's a compass and I'm due north.

I smooth bubbles up and down his shaft until precum weeps from the top, mixing with the suds. I drop the sponge to stroke him in earnest, starting at the base and twisting each time I reach the head. His grip on my ass gets harsher, and the fingers inside me falter.

"Fuuuck, Mila. You're going to make me bust if you're not careful."

I consider that. I *do* enjoy making men lose control...To prove it, I tighten my fist around his cock and stroke faster, rewarded with a full body shudder. *Yeah. That's fun.*

Plus, he's so sexy when he begs. I almost came listening to all the filthy things he whispered when I sucked his cock before. I torture him with a few more strokes, then release him. Maybe another time.

Instead, I tear open the foil packet and roll the condom down his stiff length. I plant my knees on either side of his hips on the bench, grab hold of his shoulders, and slowly lower myself. I tease his tip against my lips first, smiling at Henry's gasp. All he can do is hang on as I lower my pussy onto his dick with excruciating slowness. I hear the longing and desire in his keening moan and start bouncing in his lap, angling his cock so it hits my G-spot every time my ass meets his thighs.

His eyes roll back in his head, and my inner succubus takes over. I bounce faster, clenching my pussy around his cock when I reach the base and squeezing the whole way up.

"Oh God, oh God, oh God," he groans, seemingly sense-less. *That's more like it.*

With a move I know will break him, I reach back and cup his balls from behind my back.

"Oh, fuck!!"

He grunts his release, warmth filling the condom as his cock throbs inside of me. The desperate jerks of his hips trigger my own orgasm, and my pussy flutters around his length, dragging a final stream from his cock. We collapse together, both wrung out from the intensity of our joining.

"Holy shit, Mila. You were trying to take my soul with that one."

I wink.

"Maybe a little."

We take turns drying each other off, and Henry hands me a terrycloth robe from behind the door.

"Just until we can head into town tomorrow and get you some clothes." I raise an eyebrow and step into the robe as he holds it open.

"I'm staying over tonight, too?"

Henry wraps the belt around my middle and pulls it tight. My boobs threaten to spill out of the soft material.

"Of course. I told you I can hardly sleep without you."

I follow him back into the bedroom, where he steps into pajama bottoms, leaving his chest bare. He pierces me with a look that says he's already ready for another round, but I turn from his gaze and head towards the stairs.

"Where are you going?" he asks, his voice laced with worry.

"I just slept for twenty-four hours and then we fucked like rabbits. I need food."

His shoulders sag in relief and his lips quirk up in amusement.

"Oh. Right."

CHAPTER THIRTY-ONE

Epilogue

HENRY

Two weeks later...

I should've broken these shoes in more. My feet are killing me. I grin through my discomfort and survey the lavish surroundings. Though we're in the middle of the city with skyscrapers looming over us, the manicured gardens, reflecting pool, and fountains on the rooftop of 620 Loft & Garden make it feel like we're in the Red Queen's court from *Alice in Wonderland*. Rows of gold Chiavari chairs sit on each side of an aisle covered in freshly sprinkled rose petals. One of Maya's students from the community center in Harlem served as the flower girl. A harpist plucks Pachelbel's Canon in D as we process in and take our positions to the left and right of the altar.

My brothers and I look like we walked straight out of Korean Vogue in sharp, black tuxes, but Adam's custom velvet suit stands out against our rentals. He looks good; you can hardly tell he's still hungover from our booze cruise down the Hudson River two days ago.

Across the aisle, the bridesmaids wear royal blue strapless gowns with corsages of blue and white flowers that match our boutonnieres. Mom and Dad wear blue too, and both have flowers to match the rest of the wedding party. The blue is an homage to our Korean heritage: blue signifies the balance of yin and yang, two forces that complement and attract each other.

I scan the row behind Mom and Dad until I meet familiar brown eyes and my breath catches. Camila is literally breathtaking. She's wearing blue too, though not the same shade as the wedding party. I surprised her with a couture gown from Marchesa that hugs her voluptuous hips and accentuates her full breasts. I can't wait to get her out of it later.

She catches me staring and blows me a kiss. I pretend to catch it and put it in my pocket and she giggles. It feels so good to have someone to be silly with. Before I can continue flirting, she discreetly points to the aisle just as the harpist switches to Wagner's Bridal Chorus.

The crowd turns to watch Maya's grand entrance. She's a vision in white. Her dress reminds me of Cinderella's, with a full skirt and a train over ten feet long, though her neckline's showing far more cleavage than any Disney movie would allow. *Our baby brother did well!*

Maya's eyes are shining with happy tears and glued to the head of the aisle. I follow her gaze to find Adam looking completely awestruck. The love arching between them can be felt by everyone in attendance, and it makes the love I feel for Camila swell even bigger in my chest. It's not hard to imagine she and I tying the knot, and I look for her to find her already looking at me. The love is so clear on her face, she may as well have hearts in her eyes.

Once the I do's are done, we move inside to the elegantly appointed banquet hall. I have to sit at the head table with the rest of the wedding party, but luckily, Maya managed to squeeze Camila into a table up front, where we can stare at each other until the dance floor finally opens.

Dings from a knife against a water glass get everyone's attention and Maya's father stands from a table at the front of the room. He's a formidable man at over six feet, and almost a dead ringer for Blade. Like my father, he keeps himself up, but he's much more fashionable, sporting a navy, three-piece suit with a steel gray cravat. I met him for the first time at the rehearsal dinner last night, and I was more than a little intimidated.

"Good evening, everyone," he says with a voice so smooth and deep, he could give James Earl Jones a run for his money. He hardly even needs the mic. All remaining chatter in the room ceases.

"On behalf of the bride and groom, thank you for coming to celebrate this momentous occasion. For those that don't know,

I'm Michael Davis, father of the bride." In the center of the head table, Maya is glowing with pride for her father.

"We'll get a chance to cut a rug later, but, for now, it's time for the speeches." Michael takes a paper out of his breast pocket and clears his throat.

"When Adam came to visit Evelyn and I—" He points to a regal woman that could be the queen from "Coming to America". "Evelyn is my lovely wife and Maya's mother. Anyway, when Adam came to meet with us to ask for Maya's hand, we were a little skeptical. He and Maya hadn't been dating for very long, and they met through the internet, although thank God it wasn't a dating app!" Laughter spreads through the audience and Maya covers her face in embarrassment.

"Dad!" More laughter from the crowd.

"We weren't sure if they really knew what they were getting into, and not just because of how fast they wanted to get married." His face turns serious.

"I look around this room and can guess that almost everyone has experienced the harsh judgments of those with different backgrounds and different viewpoints." Mutterings of agreement come from the crowd. "Those judgments can become almost overwhelming when two people such as Maya and Adam come together."

I look at the happy couple and they are staring into each other's eyes, hands clasped together.

"But even though there's no way a mother or father can protect their daughter from life's sometimes cruel treatment, we knew after talking to him and looking into his eyes that Adam is a truly good man. He loves our daughter and will do everything in his power to protect her. Together, they will weather any storm. A father couldn't wish for anything more in a son-in-law."

There's not a dry eye in the room, and even Cory is blinking back tears.

"So raise your glasses," he says. Everywhere around us, glasses arc raised high in the air. "To Maya and Adam! May their marriage be long and healthy, and may the skies always be clear!"

Everyone drinks and cheers. Adam and Maya embrace, sharing a loving kiss. Evelyn pats her husband on the back. I look at Camila and find her dabbing her eyes with a dinner napkin. Dancing can't come soon enough.

The speeches conclude, dinner is served, the cake is cut, and finally, *finally*, my duties as a groomsman are done. I scoot behind my brothers' chairs to the dance floor and weave between other guests to stand in front of Camila. She's currently trapped talking to my chattiest relative, Aunt Soo Yun.

"A lawyer? Really?," Aunt Soo Yun coos. Outside of her line of sight, Mila begs me to rescue her with her eyes. I chuckle under my breath.

"Auntie, how are you?!" I lean down to give her a kiss on the cheek. "You look lovely. Do you have your eye on any lucky bachelors tonight?"

She playfully swats my arm for being fresh, but preens under my compliment, nonetheless.

"Oh, Henry. You always were incorrigible." I wink at her and gesture towards my date for the night.

"Do you mind if I steal Ms. Sanchez from you? After making her wait through the ceremony, I owe her a dance." Aunt Soo Yun smiles slyly.

"Of course!" She urges Camila out of her seat and into my arms. On the way out to the dance floor, I call back over my shoulder.

"Don't break too many hearts tonight, Auntie!" She laughs and shoos me away like I'm being ridiculous.

The DJ has perfect timing, putting on a slow song as soon as we find a place on the dance floor. I pull Mila tighter into my arms, one hand on the small of her back and the other holding her hand.

"Have I told you how ravishing you look tonight?" She giggles as I lead her into a twirl.

"Ravishing? Did we suddenly teleport into a Jane Austen novel?"

"Jane Austen's characters never did half the things we did last night," I say with a devilish smirk. Her cheeks turn the most charming pink and I can't help but give her a quick kiss.

"Have I told you 'thank you' for being my date tonight?"

"Yes," she murmurs against my chest, snuggling deeper into my arms. "Once last night, when we were..." She trails off and blushes again. "And once when I got here, before you were whisked off to join the wedding party.

I take a deep breath. Here comes the moment of truth.

"And have I told you I love you?" I ask. My heart is pounding, and Camila stops swaying to the music, eyes wide. "It's pretty obvious. I've hardly been hiding it, but I wanted to say the words."

Her face lights up into a smile that reaches ear to ear, and she stands on her tippy toes to kiss me.

"I love you too, Henry!" she says, her voice breathless. My heart resumes beating.

"Oh, thank God!" I sigh, and we both laugh, relieved to have everything out in the open.

"Since we're official—"

"And officially in love!" Mila interrupts, still smiling wide.

"Yes, love," I say, giving her another small kiss. "Since we're officially in love, would you like to meet my family?" Her shoulders tense the tiniest bit, and I pull her even tighter against me. "Don't worry. They're going to love you as much as I do. I promise."

I don't wait for an answer, but instead pull her towards the nearest free relatives: Mom and Dad. Mom spots us as we approach and stands with her arms outstretched.

"You must be the illustrious Camila! I was hoping I'd get to meet you!" She pulls Camila in for a hug and I laugh at her nervous expression.

"Hello, Mrs. Park," she says once Mom releases her. "It's a pleasure to meet you. The wedding is truly stunning." Mom pats her arm.

"Thank you, dear, and please, call me Marie. I had a small hand in the planning—Adam is our youngest, you know—but the vision was all Maya's." She looks wistfully out at the room.

"Well, it might be the fanciest wedding I've ever been to," Camila answers, some of the nervousness leaving her voice. From behind Mom, Dad steps forward and takes Mila's hand.

"I'm so glad to meet you, Ms. Sanchez. I hear you're going to be a lawyer?" Mila looks down before grinning shyly.

"Fingers crossed," she says, and I squeeze her hand. "I just took the bar two weeks ago."

"And she aced it," I add adamantly. Mom and Dad look between us and smile knowingly.

"Well, if you have my son Junior here's stamp of approval," he roughly shakes my shoulders in a masculine display of camaraderie, "you must have a helluva legal mind on those shoulders." Camila blushes at the compliment.

Before we can turn to leave, Noah, Damon and Cory join us at the table.

"Is this Camila?" Damon asks, stealing shrimp from Mom's plate. He's the giant of the family and he's always hungry. I'm so glad he could make it home for the wedding. I almost laugh at Camila's stunned expression.

"Uh, yes? Are you Henry's other brothers?" she asks? Damon smiles and motions first to himself, then to Cory.

"In the flesh. I'm Damon, the one who plays ball overseas. And this is our ne'er-do-well brother, Cory. He makes his money trading crypto and schmoozing with Finance bros all day. I think you already know Noah."

Noah lifts his glass in Mila's direction and Cory glares at Damon before reaching out to shake Camila's hand.

"Good to meet you, Camila. My jock brother has clearly been hit too many times by foul balls. I trade *options*, not crypto. I work for Banks Ripley, the hedge fund." Camila smiles blankly, clearly overwhelmed by all the Park brothers surrounding her. I pull her closer to my side.

"It looks like you have the girl surrounded," Maya laughs, coming up to the table with Adam to make it a full family affair. Camila's eyes almost bug out of her head.

"Wow. Hi Maya! Thank you so much for letting me come to your wedding. I was just telling Mrs. Park—" Camila catches herself. "Well, I guess *you're* Mrs. Park now, too." Adam squeezes Maya around the waist as she beams.

"I was just telling your mother-in-law how beautiful the ceremony was. This venue is amazing. I'll probably have a courthouse wedding, myself," Camila jokes, and Mom gasps.

"You wouldn't *dare*! Henry is my eldest. You wouldn't deny a mother her right to spoil her eldest son on his wedding day, would you?"

Mila opens and closes her mouth like a fish while Noah tries to cover his laugh with a cough. I just smile, aware Mom's not too far off base. I'll convince Camila soon enough.

"Thanks for introducing yourselves and simultaneously scaring the shit out of Camila, everyone," I jokingly scold. My brothers smirk but Dad has a stern expression.

"Language, son."

"Sorry, Dad," I apologize. "If you'll excuse us, we're headed back to the dance floor."

Mila waves as I lead her away, looking like she's just been through a whirlwind.

"You'll get used to them," I say warmly, loving the feel of her supple curves against me. *Is it rude for a groomsman to leave early?* Maya waves me off like I'm being ridiculous.

"They're great, Henry," she says, and I let out a breath I didn't know I was holding. "Your family is just so much *bigger* than my little trio with Rory and Gabe. It was a tad overwhelming all at once."

"There are a lot of us, but we're very close. After a few family dinners, you'll be making fun of Cory and Damon along with the rest of us." She sighs dreamily and the thought of her joining our family melts my heart.

"I can't wait," she whispers.

Acknowledgements

As always, I want to thank my amazing husband, Calvin Wright. He is my support system, my biggest cheerleader, and he also came through with *amazing* cover art when my last designer fell through. He stepped up without even asking and was so accommodating of my many notes and changes. The cover is a book's first impression, and because of him, it's a great one.

I want to thank everyone who made *Champagne Kisses* a success. Because of you, The Park Brothers will all have their stories told, and I get to say I'm a real indie author!

To my fellow writers on the many Discord servers and Reddit forums on which I participate, thank you for your invaluable feedback, and for being a constant source of knowledge, laughter, and solidarity in this crazy life we've chosen. I wouldn't be able to do any of this without these amazing communities.

Also by Katherine E. Webb

The Park Brothers Series

Champagne Kisses

Pride & Precedents

About the Author

The epitome of a late bloomer, Katherine managed her near constant sexual frustration as an adolescent by writing spicy romance shorts to entertain herself and her close friends. This hobby continued into college, where she began posting her shorts to a blog no one visited.

Many years later, when her mother lost her battle to cancer, Katherine inherited a Kindle fully loaded with romance novels. Katherine decided to read all the stories loaded onto the eReader to feel closer to her late mother, ultimately reigniting her passion for steamy love stories and inspiring her to write her own. Her work will always feature characters with experiences and viewpoints which are often underrepresented in mainstream romance.

Katherine holds a degree in English and an MBA. Based in Houston, TX, she's a wife and mom to a gifted young man and two cats. When she's not writing, Katherine spends her limited free time reading romance novels, watching the latest entry into the MCU, and predicting the ending to Hallmark movies.

Keep in touch with Katherine and hear about current and upcoming releases on Instagram (@KatWroteThat).

www.ingramcontent.com/pod-product-compliance
Lightning Source LLC
Chambersburg PA
CBHW031249160726
47993CB00001B/80